Lily's in London?!

Other Books Available

The Lily Series

Here's Lily!

Lily Robbins, M.D. (Medical Dabbler)

Lily and the Creep

Lily's Ultimate Party

Ask Lily

Lily the Rebel

Lights, Action, Lily!

Lily Rules!

Rough & Rugged Lily

Lily Speaks!

Horse Crazy Lily

Lily's Church Camp Adventure

Lily's in London?!

Lily's Passport to Paris

Nonfiction

The Beauty Book

The Body Book

The Buddy Book

The Best Bash Book

The Blurry Rules Book

The It's MY Life Book

The Creativity Book

The Uniquely Me Book

The Year 'Round Holiday Book

The Values & Virtues Book

The Fun-Finder Book

The Walk-the-Walk Book

NIV Young Women of Faith Bible

the Lily series

Lily's in London?!

Nancy Rue

zonderkidz

ZONDERVAN.com/
AUTHORTRACKER
follow your favorite authors

The children's group of Zondervan

www.zonderkidz.com

Requests for information should be addressed to:
Zonderkidz, Grand Rapids, Michigan 49530

ISBN-13: 978-0-310-70554-1
ISBN-10: 0-310-70554-1

Published in association with the literary agency of Alive Communications, Inc., 7680 Goddard Street, Suite 200, Colorado Springs, CO 80920. www.alivecommunications.com

Editor: Barbara J. Scott
Interior design: Amy Langeler
Cover design: Jody Langley

Printed in the United States of America

07 08 09 10 11 12 • 15 14 13 12 11 10 9

Chapter **1**

All right, Lilianna," Mudda said. "Enough partying. It's time to get down to some serious business."

Lily Robbins felt her blue eyes widening as she stared into her grandmother's face. Around her the party crowd on the deck seemed to hold its breath, as if everyone were using the same pair of lungs. Forks full of potato salad stopped midair.

"What do you mean, 'enough partying,' Mudda?"

That came from Lily's ten-year-old adopted sister, Tessa, who hadn't been in the family long enough to be used to calling her new grandmother "Mudda," the way Lily and her brothers did. Tessa's mossy green eyes narrowed just as dramatically as, Lily knew, her own were popping out of her head. Lily tugged nervously at one of the curls that had escaped from her wild red ponytail.

"I thought this was all about Lily tonight," Tessa said. She started to curl her lip. "How come you're saying she has to do some stupid serious thing?"

Lily heard her father whisper, "Watch your tone, Tess," but Tessa was fearless in the face of the sometimes-grumpy Mudda, who was looking particularly disgruntled at the moment—until Lily saw the glimmer in her bright-blue eyes, which meant she was probably up to something. Lily's mother had obviously caught on too, because she elbowed Mudda, her ponytail bouncing. Mudda's hair, in its crisply cut, gray helmet style, didn't budge an inch.

"Come on, Mudda—what's this serious business?" Mom said.

"Well, presents, of course," Mudda said. "I saw them stacked in the family room like the Leaning Tower of Pisa. I think it's time we got to them before they fall over."

"Yes!" Tessa bounded toward the back door.

"Man," said Lily's eleven-year-old brother, Joe. "I never saw a chick who could change moods so fast."

"Unlike you," Art said, "who's been in the same foul mood for two weeks."

That was true, Lily thought. Joe *had* been walking around with his lip practically trailing on the carpet for days, his eyebrows down to his upper lip in a scowl that seemed to be pasted permanently onto his face with Superglue. Still, Lily had also noticed that lately her brother Art, who was almost eighteen, was making more and more comments that sounded as if they ought to be coming out of a grown-up's mouth.

"He's seventeen going on forty," she had heard Mom say to Dad.

Well, duh, Lily thought. *Because he's the one who's getting to stay in his own hometown and at his own school, while the rest of us go thousands of miles away, where we don't know anybody, where people aren't even Americans— and for a whole year!*

"You comin', Lil?"

Lily looked up to discover that the only person left on the back deck with her was her best friend, Reni, standing with her hands on her hips.

"You don't look that thrilled about opening your presents," Reni said. "What's the deal?"

Lily gazed at her in surprise. Reni was definitely her best friend of all the Girlz, but she wasn't usually this sympathetic. Her very black eyes looked bigger than ever, framed by her tight cornrows of hair, and they actually looked sad. It took a lot to make Reni sad. But then, this was a lot. Lily stood up and started for the back door.

"I'd be more thrilled if they weren't *going-away* presents," Lily said. "I don't wanna go to England, Reni. I mean, I do, because Dad wants us to. But I don't want to leave you."

"I don't want you to go, either," Reni said, swallowing hard. "I don't think I'll be able to stand it without you."

"But you'll still have Kresha and Suzy and Zooey—"

"They aren't you!"

"But Reni," Lily said, "I won't have *anybody*."

Reni got another huge gulp down past the lump in her throat and then folded her arms across her chest as if she were warding off a blizzard.

"Okay, we gotta stop this," she said. "You're always gonna have us. We're gonna email you, like, six times a day and—"

"It won't be the same," Lily said, "and you know it."

"Lee-Lee?"

They both turned to see Kresha peering at them through the screen door, her nose pressed against the mesh as though she were six years old. To Lily, it was as if they were all little kids now, each one of them on the verge of a tantrum.

"Your grandmudda—she says she will open the presents her own self if you not come."

Lily straightened her shoulders. If Kresha, who was Croatian but spoke almost perfect English now, was slipping back into her old butchered sentences, she really was feeling bad. Lily pulled open the door and put her arm around Kresha's thin little shoulders.

"No way she's opening my presents," Lily said.

"Yes, way."

"I believe it," Reni said. "I'm still scared of that lady."

As if to prove it, Reni hurried ahead of them through the dining room and into the family room. But Lily lagged behind a little in the kitchen, dragging her fingers across the back of one of the chairs.

"Hey, Kresh?" she said.

"Yeah, Lee-Lee?"

"What was it like for you, coming to a foreign country?"

"You mean America?"

"Yeah."

"But America is my home now!"

"I know—but when you first came, was it scary?"

Kresha nodded solemnly. Her sparkly eyes seemed to be remembering things as they peered through her bangs.

"I could not understand what people were saying," Kresha said. "I don't know—didn't know—what were the rules in school, and ..."

"And what?"

"Everybody made fun of me when I tried to talk in English." Her eyes perked up suddenly. "Until you, Lee-Lee—and the Girlz Only! You change everything for me."

Just as suddenly as she'd started to smile, Kresha's face crumpled and she threw her arms around Lily's neck. Lily hugged her and thought, *There won't be any Girlz Only Club in Oxford to help me. I'm going to have to take the teasing and the rules and all that stuff all by myself.*

"Are we crying?" asked a voice from the dining room doorway.

Lily looked over Kresha's trembling shoulder at Zooey, her round-faced friend who, she knew, could melt into tears on a second's notice, especially if one of the other Girlz was doing it. Lily swallowed the lump in her throat that threatened to turn the whole scene into a crying marathon, and let go of Kresha.

"Not anymore," Lily said. She gave Kresha a nudge and heard her noisily snuff the rest of her own tears up through her nose. "We're done. Did they start without me?"

"Not yet," Zooey said. "But Tessa's about to wet her pants. It's a good thing she had her party last week or she'd be climbing the wall."

As if on cue, Tessa suddenly appeared above Zooey, atop the shoulders of Shad Shifferdecker.

"Don't bang my head, Shifferdecker," Tessa said, ducking her short, dark-haired head to keep from hitting the top of the doorway.

Lily saw Zooey stiffen out of habit. After all, Shad *had* been a permanent pain in the neck to the Girlz all through sixth grade. But Lily grinned at him. After seventh grade he'd turned out to be not so bad. She could actually stand him now that he no longer called her "Robbins" as if the word meant "goose

8

poop." He still called her "Robbins," but it was different now. In fact, she'd confided to Art just a few days earlier that Shad was starting to grow on her.

"Like a fungus between your toes," Art had said. After she'd popped him one, he got a little serious and said, "You've probably got a crush on him."

"I *so* do not!" Lily had practically shrieked.

"Methinks the lady doth protest too much," had been his answer.

That's what she meant by Art talking as if he were this adult or something. He was even *looking* older, in a thin, pasty kind of way.

She looked now at Shad and stifled a sigh. It didn't matter whether she actually had a crush on him or not, because by the time she got back—in a *year*—he would have forgotten what her name was. Period.

"Hey, Robbins," he said. "I can't keep my girlfriend here under control much longer—and I am not *even* dealing with that Mudda woman."

Suzy squeezed her head between Shad and the door frame and said, "You'd better hurry, Lily, or she really *is* gonna get mad."

Suzy always thought everybody was going to get mad, Lily knew. That was just Suzy. But Lily herded the whole group through the dining room anyway. One more second with her friends and she was going to start the kind of crying that wouldn't stop, no matter what you did. Besides, Reni's dad was there with his camera, and Lily definitely didn't want all the photos of her going-away party to show her with snot running out of her nose.

Mudda gave her a friendly scowl when she got to the family room, and pointed to the big La-Z-Boy chair next to the stack of presents, which had shifted considerably to the right. Lily was sure Tessa had been poking at them.

"Sit!" Mudda said. "Before the crowd goes mad!"

As Lily sank into the chair, she looked at the "crowd" around her. Just about everyone she loved was there—Mrs. Reinhold, her English teacher; Ed and Victoria, the two college kids who coached the Shakespeare Club; and Mr. Miniver, a man she could barely get through a day without because he was the best counselor in the *entire* middle school world. Even Herbie, from the Double H Stables, was there, although he hadn't brought Big Jake, her favorite horse on the planet. Lily had already said good-bye to him. Talk about some snot on *that* occasion.

9

Of course there were her Girlz, who right now she couldn't even look at for fear of losing it completely. She looked instead at Joe, who had already had his going-away party last weekend, attended by every kid in Burlington, New Jersey, he'd ever played baseball, basketball, or soccer with. He'd had fun at *his* party—but right after that he'd started setting the record for long-term sulking. Lily knew he was as bummed about leaving the sweaty little eleven-year-olds he was always punching as she was about leaving the Girlz she shared absolutely everything with. Maybe she shouldn't look at him after all.

She turned to her presents.

"Finally!" Tessa said. "You want me to help you?"

Lily wrinkled her nose at her. "Let me think about it—NO," she said.

"Brat," Tessa said back.

Nobody said anything. "Brat" was far better than any of the things she'd called Lily when she'd first come to live with the Robbinses. Besides, Lily knew she didn't mean it at all. Tessa was in fact the only one of the three Robbins kids going to England who was excited about it. She hadn't been able to stop talking about it for a month, and most of that had been questions fired at Lily. The child could quiz worse than Mrs. Reinhold.

"Guess who this one's from?" Tessa said, thrusting a small rectangular package onto Lily's lap.

"What is she, clairvoyant?" Art said. "Let her open the card."

While Tessa cross-examined Art on what *clairvoyant* meant, Lily read the card from Mrs. Reinhold. She had written,

> *Write down every detail that touches you. Don't trust your-
> self to remember—and you will want to remember.*

Though Lily doubted that, she did like the leather journal and the accompanying silver pen. She'd never owned anything but plastic gel pens in colors Mrs. Reinhold would never let them use to write their papers. Though now it wouldn't matter what color she wrote in, since Mom was going to be home-schooling her and Joe and Tessa. Another weird change.

Lily decided it was best to keep focusing on the presents. There was a scrapbook from the Girlz so when she came back, they could see every single thing she'd done.

"Take pictures of Big Ben and the queen and everything!" Zooey said.

"Those are in London—we're living in Oxford," Lily said.

"But you must go to London," Mrs. Reinhold said, nodding her head at Mudda as if they were thinking with the same brain.

Mudda agreed with a nod of her gray helmet-head. "London was made for you, Lilianna," she said. "Joanna, Paul—you must see that she gets there."

"What about me?" Tessa asked.

"I'm not sure whether London is ready for you, Tess," Dad said.

Ed and Victoria gave Lily a book on the new Globe Theatre in London so she'd be ready to go see some real Shakespeare. They were obviously pushing London too. It gave Lily the first glimmer of excitement she'd felt since the gloom had set in. That might not be *so* bad. A place made for her.

Mr. Miniver's present was a funny book on English slang.

"You'll pick it up straight away on your own," Mr. M. said, faking a British accent that came out of his nose. "But this should give you a leg up, right?"

"What's he talking about?" Tessa asked.

Lily had no idea and that scared her all over again.

After she opened the package of four disposable cameras from Shad, Art wiggled his eyebrows at her from across the room and mouthed the word *romantic*. Lily ignored him and turned to her last present from Mudda.

Tessa couldn't hold herself back any longer and proceeded to help Lily rip the paper off. Inside was a small canvas bag with pockets and a shoulder strap. It was khaki and cool-looking—not exactly the kind of present she would have expected from Mudda. She was more the sensible underwear-and-socks type.

"The instructions are inside," Mudda said. "You can read them later."

"Read them now!" Tessa said.

She leaped at Lily, arms flailing at the bag. When Lily pulled it out of her reach, Shad snatched it and held it above Tessa's head.

Before she could start to bellow—as only Tessa could—Mom stood and said to Zooey's mother, "Didn't you bring some kind of scrumptious dessert?"

Tessa was immediately all over that, particularly since there was chocolate involved. Lily could barely get down two bites, even though there were also raspberries and whipped cream on the concoction. Zooey's mom knew those were her favorites, because she had fixed her so many snacks down in the Girlz Only room in Zooey's basement. The thought gave Lily another stab of sadness.

It was hard to say good-bye to people she knew she wouldn't see for a year. But it was harder yet to part with the Girlz, even though they would probably be with her every possible minute for the next five days and were even going to the Philadelphia airport to see the Robbins family off.

Every time I say good-bye to them now, Lily wrote in her talking-to-God journal that night, *it brings me one good-bye closer to really leaving them. I don't know if I can do this, God!*

Tears trailed down her cheeks and this time she let them come, nose goop and all. No one was there to see it except her big stuffed panda, China, and of course, Otto. Her little mutt-dog put his gray muzzle between his two front paws and looked up at her as if he knew she was about to abandon him to the Dooleys, the family Art was going to be staying with.

"Don't bite anybody over there, okay?" Lily said to him. "I don't want them sending you back to the pound. You only have to be good for a year."

Lily leaned hard into China, because he too was staying behind. She'd tried to convince her parents to take him along, by insisting that she would hold him on her lap on the plane. But since he could easily have taken up a whole seat by himself, Mom had put the kibosh on that.

I don't think they know what they're asking me to give up, she wrote. *My room already looks like a jail cell.*

She glanced around at the now bare walls, so recently covered with her horse poster and drawings, her giant picture of Shakespeare, the certificates that proclaimed she had been president of the seventh-grade class and a finalist in the county speech contest, and all her photographs — of the Girlz and her friends at camp. A pastor on furlough from some mission in Africa was going to be staying in their house with his family while the Robbinses were gone, so Mom had strongly suggested that Lily strip her walls and shelves and pack her personal things away.

I can't even take stuff with me for my room in Oxford, she complained to God. *I know — I'm whining. I should be grateful for this opportunity. And I can't hurt Dad's feelings — he thinks this year is going to change all our lives in some big-deal way or something. But I like my life just fine the way it is, and I just know I'm going to be so lonely — even worse than when I first went to summer camp.*

Her eyes fell on the canvas bag Mudda had given her. That, she had instructed, Lily *must* take with her. Lily picked it up and dug out the instructions her grandmother had folded inside.

Mudda had written,

> *This is your pilgrimage bag. Before you leave for Great Britain, fill one sandwich bag with New Jersey dirt from your backyard. Tuck another empty bag into one of these pockets. As you travel, always pick up a little of the soil from each special place you go and leave a few grains of yours in its place. I think you will learn along the way what significance this has. You are a smart girl. After all, you are my granddaughter.*

Lily snickered a little through her tears.

> *Might I also suggest that you keep a camera, a journal, and a pen in this bag. There will be so much to savor, Lilianna. It doesn't seem so now, when you are mourning having to leave the only home you've ever known and friends who are so dear to you. But no pilgrimage that God sends you on is too much for God to ask of you. It will be worth the tears you are shedding now.*

> *I love you. Godspeed.*
> *Mudda*

Lily put the note down, buried her face in China, and sobbed.

"I hope you know what you're doing, God," she cried into China's matted fur, while Otto licked the back of her neck. "Just please be my friend while I'm off on this pilgrimage. I need you."

And then she cried herself to sleep.

Chapter 2

I feel like I've been shot and I've just forgotten to fall down," Lily's mom said.

Lily squinted at her through the fog of English air. "You kind of look a little like that too, Mom," she said.

In fact, gazing at the bags under her mother's eyes, which seemed almost as large as the luggage they were currently dragging out of the Oxford train station, Lily decided maybe it was worse than that. Pieces of Mom's usually smooth ponytail were standing out like broom straws, and the khakis she'd been wearing for the last twenty-four hours were creased across her lap in stiff wrinkles. Everything from Tessa's ketchup to Joe's fourteenth Coke had been spilled all over them.

But who wouldn't look that way? Lily thought. After ten hours on airplanes, they'd spent two hours in lines at the airport in London, with people pawing through every one of their fifteen suitcases and talking in their snippy little way. Oh, and after the two and a half hours on the train to Oxford, squished between Tessa, who wouldn't shut up, and Joe, who wouldn't say anything—after all that, Lily was sure she looked even worse than her mother.

But before Lily had a chance to turn around and gaze at herself in the glass doors they'd just managed to get through, Dad trotted up from around the corner. His eyes were saggy too, his glasses were smeary, and his shirttail was coming out. But he had the same flushed cheeks and look of adventure that Tessa did. She was right at his heels.

"We found taxis!" she bellowed.

Several people, who all seemed to be wearing black and had faces the color of cream of wheat, turned to stare. Lily had already noticed that mostly, the English people didn't yell. Every time Tessa had laughed out loud on the train, at least one person had given Mom a look that seemed to say, "Could you please muzzle that child?"

"Right around the corner," Dad said. "You can just roll right down this ramp. I had to get two cabs."

"Ya think?" Joe muttered. That was only the second thing he had said to Lily since they left Philadelphia. The first was, "I'm really over this whole England thing." That was two minutes after they landed.

"Wait till you see these taxicabs, Lily!" Tessa said as she fell into step beside her, dragging two wheeled bags. "They're all black and big and weird lookin', and they have the steering wheels on the wrong side, just like in those books we looked at!"

"Remember what Dad said," Lily told her. "We're not supposed to say they do it 'wrong.' We're supposed to try to accept their culture."

"Is that what you're doin'?" Tessa asked.

Her intense green eyes were studying Lily's face — a face, Lily knew, that didn't look a whole lot happier than Joe's. Lily could feel her mother looking at her, so she said, "Yeah, that's what I'm trying to do. Start by keeping your voice down. Everybody's looking."

But Tessa went on to talking loudly about the proper-looking cab drivers — who looked to Lily as if they'd been sucking on lemons — and about the exit signs, which Tessa found hilarious. They showed little figures dashing off as if they were running from snakes.

Lily was relieved to finally get into the cab so the only person staring at them was the driver, who did so rather disapprovingly in the rearview mirror.

Lily didn't know whether to ask him to please mind his own business, or to stuff a sock into Tessa's mouth.

She did neither, however, because before she could decide, they were suddenly slowing at the curb of a busy street in front of a house.

"Number five Woodstock Road," the cab driver said.

Lily was sure she heard a little relief in his voice, which she forgot the minute she got her first real look at the house—the house they were going to be living in for a year.

"Well, that's … quaint," Mom said.

"What's *quaint* mean?" Tessa asked.

Dad, who had already seen the place on his last trip to England, had described it to them as "a marvelous two-story full of English character." Lily was pretty sure that Mom's calling it "quaint" was a nice way of saying Dad had exaggerated a little. *How 'bout a lot!* Lily thought.

The house looked like a big cream-colored box with windows and a narrow roof. There was no porch, no lawn—just a small triangle of overhang attempting to shelter the black front door. There was a window on each side downstairs with white shutters that made the whole thing look milky and colorless.

"It's a big ol' square of white chocolate!" Tessa said.

"How poetic, Tess," Dad said.

He reached into the backseat of the cab to help Mom out. All traces of travel fatigue were gone from his face, and he looked to Lily as if he were about to pop with a long-kept secret.

"Well, what do you think?" he asked.

"Which one of those rooms is mine?" Tessa asked. She pointed to the three shutterless windows on the second floor.

"That one on the end is your father's and mine, I can tell you that right now," Mom said, nodding at the soot-stained chimney that topped it, "because that's where the fireplace is."

"Is there another bedroom in the back?" Lily asked.

"No," Dad said.

Mom was watching Lily closely. "I think that means you and Tessa will be sharing a room."

16

"That rocks!" Tessa said. "I wanna see it!"

She crawled over Lily to get out of the cab. Although the driver already had all the bags dumped onto the sidewalk, Lily wished she could just ride back to the airport with him.

This gets worse by the minute, she thought. She loved Tessa, but the idea of living in the same room with her for a whole year was right up there with playing marathon dodgeball for the same amount of time. She could already hear the questions and the endless stream of comments like, "Lily, let's read that part again" and "It's no fair that you get to stay up later, wear earrings, and use lip gloss." She felt herself cringe.

Things didn't get much better when they went inside. The black door led to an even blacker short entrance hall, until Dad pulled a chain and a stark lightbulb went on over their heads.

"Charming," Mom muttered.

Tessa tore into the room on the right, which, Lily discovered as she followed her, was a living room with a lumpy beige sofa and stiff-looking brown leather chairs that had a lot of brass tacks around the edges. The walls were covered entirely by bookshelves crammed full all the way to the ceiling. Lily figured that was probably why there was a ladder that could slide completely around the room.

Mom tapped it and looked at Tessa. "This is off-limits to you and Joe."

"No fair!" Tessa said.

Joe didn't seem to care. He turned from the corner of the room and said, "Is this, like, the oldest television left on the planet?"

"I think so!" Dad said cheerfully.

For once, Lily felt Joe's moaning wasn't an exaggeration. There was a tiny TV set atop a crocheted cloth on a table in the darkest corner of the room, with antennae sticking out of it like two big victory fingers.

"You won't be able to see that TV from any of the chairs!" Joe said.

Lily looked down at the floor, the next logical TV-watching place, but it was bare wood and it looked cold, even in late August.

Mom opened the beige — of course — curtains, letting in some sun. Such as there was. The light seemed thin to Lily.

"You have to remember that Dr. Sheggs is a bachelor," Dad was saying to Mom. "I'm sure the digs he's living in down in South America aren't as comfortable as this."

Lily shuddered for the poor man.

"Hey, look in here!" Tessa called from across the hall.

They all hurried after her, as if they were grateful to leave the depressing little living room. What they walked into was grand by comparison — a dining room with faded wallpaper that looked as if it had once had a raised pattern on it, and a thick heavy table surrounded by chairs padded in deep maroon.

"It's going to take a forklift to pull one of those out from the table," Mom said. She grinned at Dad. "You expecting to entertain much?"

Dad opened the glass-fronted china cabinet with a flourish. "He said we were welcome to use all this china and crystal."

Mom looked at Tessa.

"I know," Tessa said. "That's off-limits to me and Joe."

"Like I even want to touch any of that junk," Joe said. "Can I go up to my room now and put my stuff away?"

"Don't you want to see the rest of the house?" Dad asked.

He looked a little disappointed and Lily felt a pang for him.

"I do, Dad," she said.

Dad recovered his grin and led Mom, Lily, and Tessa down another dark hall into a huge kitchen. It had white walls that looked as if they'd just been freshly painted, which helped — although somebody had talked the poor man into trimming the cabinets in bright blue and yellow. Lily was pretty sure the word for that was *garish*.

There were appliances that looked older than the ones Mudda had just given to Goodwill, and Lily didn't want to be around when Joe saw the size of the refrigerator. He thought the *television* was small!

At the other end of the kitchen was a shiny rectangular wooden table and high-backed chairs, set close to the window, where the sun was struggling to come inside. Once again Mom pulled open the curtains. They were brown-checked, and Lily could tell from the expression on her face that those babies would be coming down soon. Still, Lily hoped this was where they were going to eat most of their meals. The dining room looked as if a funeral ought to be taking place there instead of a meal.

Tessa meanwhile had just finished exploring, at one end of the table, a set of stairs that curved up into darkness.

"How come there's two sets of stairs?" she asked.

"Front stairs and back stairs," Dad said. "Probably when the house was first built, only the family and their guests could use the front stairs. The servants used the back."

"Are we gonna have servants?" Tessa asked.

"Dream on," Mom said.

"And don't expect me to pick up after you, either," Lily said. "Even if we *are* sharing a room."

"We are!" Tessa said. "I just saw it—come on!"

There was nothing Lily wanted to do less. She was trying not to be crabby, since Joe was grouchy enough for the entire family. But she was in serious need of some alone time.

"You know what," Mom said, "we have been on top of each other for twenty-four hours. What do you say all of you go find a place to veg by yourselves for a couple hours while I see if I can get this place into functioning order?"

Joe, Lily heard, had already snapped on the TV. Dad said he was going over to the college to let them know he'd arrived.

"What are you gonna do, Lily?" Tessa asked.

"Whatever it is, she isn't doing it with you," Mom said. "Everyone needs to be by themselves for a little while."

"But I wanna go with—"

"Nope. Find something to do—but don't take a nap. You'll be up all night."

"A nap!" Tessa said. "Like I would do that anyway."

As she went on to bemoan her alone-fate, Lily gave her mother a grateful look over the top of Tessa's head. Mom always got it. At least Lily hadn't had to leave *her* behind.

"I think I'll go outside," Lily said. And before Tessa could wriggle away from Mom, she hurried out the front door and stared, blinking, into the street.

Although the sun was definitely not bright, it was Miami Beach compared with how dark it was in the house.

The door opened behind her.

"You sure you don't want me to come with you?" Tessa asked.

"Yes, I'm *so* sure," Lily said.

She turned and looked at Tessa in time to see a flicker go through her little sister's eyes, something she hadn't seen in a while. Not good. That was Tessa's old angry self.

But she's gonna see worse than anger if she doesn't leave me alone for a little while, Lily thought as she stepped onto the sidewalk. *If she'll just give me some time, I'll be in a better mood.*

Of course, whether Tessa would be or not was a different story. Lily heard the door slam hard enough to rattle the windows.

Woodstock Road was four lanes with a median in the middle, but Lily decided to cross it anyway. She looked to her left to make sure no cars were coming and stepped out. A horn blared and brakes squealed—and Lily jolted around to her right to see a small truck just missing her. The driver glared, red-faced, through his side window.

"Sorry," Lily said. "But you *were* going the wrong way."

It took a second—and several more cars in his wake—for Lily to remember that they did it that way here—drove on the side of the road opposite from the one people in the United States drove on—which only made sense, since the steering wheels were on the opposite side too.

I'm never going to get used to this place, she thought.

But she managed to get herself to the other side of the street and then looked around for someplace to sit down and just *be* for a minute. She was so tired that she didn't think she could stand any longer.

The most likely looking place was a church, which Lily realized was directly across the street from their house. It wasn't like her sprawling church back in New Jersey, but that didn't surprise her. She and Tessa had been looking at pictures of England the whole summer, and Lily had been sort of intrigued by how old and fancy and kind of holy-looking the English churches were. She'd been a little excited—before it hit her how hard it was going to be to leave her own places behind.

Still, standing in front of the church now, Lily couldn't help but be fascinated all over again. In person it looked even older than in the pictures—its pale stone walls hidden amid tall trees that bent over a peaked roof. The sign said it was St. Margaret's.

A moment later Lily found herself walking down a covered walkway presided over by Christ on the cross. She pulled open a heavy door and let herself into the church.

I wonder if I'm even allowed to be in here, Lily thought. But the question faded as she gazed at what lay before her.

Straight ahead, beyond the rows of chairs on the slate floor, was an altar of shining dark wood. Behind it was a series of carved scenes on wooden panels, figures that drew her closer so she could see that they portrayed the coming of the Wise Men, Jesus' crown of thorns, and the vine that Jesus talked about. Lily stood and gazed at the figures with their haloes, and further up at the stone angels that seemed to guard it all from anyone who didn't show the proper reverence for God.

It took her a minute to figure out that she must not be alone here, since an organist was practicing and an old man with thinning white hair was polishing the sills beneath the stained-glass windows.

"I'm pretty sure you're in here, God," she whispered. "Will you tell me what *I'm* doing here?"

"Now that," someone whispered back, "is a brilliant question."

Lily whirled to see a tiny face peering at her out of the dimness.

Chapter 3

Lily gasped. She was sure she was looking at the oldest woman—oldest person—she had ever seen. Her face was wrinkled like a raisin, so that her tiny eyes were almost obscured by crinkles of skin. What Lily could see were two beams of murky amber, as if they had faded from brown years ago.

"I'm sorry!" Lily said. "I didn't know I wasn't supposed to be here—I'm not from around here."

The old woman nodded her white head as she cupped her hand around one ear. The little hair she had left waved in a feeble way across her very red scalp. Lily thought there was probably more hair in her large nose—a nose that looked like a leathery cone full of marbles as it bobbed up and down near Lily's face.

"I'm from the United States, actually," Lily blabbered on, "and we don't just go walking into any old church there, either. But they're usually locked and this one was open, so I thought—"

Lily stopped. Hand still cupping her ear, the old woman began to smile. And as she did, her face became a cobweb of ancient lines and her eyes twinkled. Lily let out a long breath.

"So it's okay that I'm here?" she asked. "Are you sure?"

The lady just continued to beam at her, long enough for Lily to notice that she seemed to have more and better teeth than had a lot of the older English people she'd seen in the airport and on the train. It changed everything, and Lily found herself smiling too, though it felt stiff, like legs she hadn't used in a while.

"I'm so glad I'm not in trouble," Lily said. "I just *got* here, like, an hour ago. I'd hate to tell my parents I'd already broken some law or something."

"Which of God's laws could you possibly have broken, my dear?" the old woman asked. "You came in asking the right question."

"Did I ask a question?"

"The right question—and of the right person."

"You?" Lily asked. She was beginning to feel a little dizzy.

"No—God. You asked him what you're doing here."

"Oh," Lily said.

Okay, she thought, *you really are a strange old woman. Now the question is, how do I get out of here?*

She was about to look ultra-casually around for a fast way to escape, when the old woman smiled again. And again Lily found herself slowly grinning back at her. Her ears echoed with every warning her parents had ever given her about talking to strangers.

"I wasn't really asking what I was doing *here,* like in this church," she said. "It was more about what I'm doing *here*—in England. See, I'm an American."

"Are you now?" The woman's eyes were sparkling, as if Lily delighted her. Lily could feel herself getting embarrassed-blotchy. She hoped the dimness covered it. Joe always said she looked as if she had a disease when her skin went that way.

"I guess you could tell that, huh?" Lily said.

"Yes. But God loves you anyway." The old lady chuckled—a surprisingly young sound compared with her crackly speaking voice—and held out her hand. "My name is Benedict. Welcome to England."

Lily knew it would be impolite not to shake this Benedict woman's hand, but it was so small and gnarled. She was half afraid it would break if she squeezed it too hard.

"I'm Lily," she said.

"Well, Lily," Benedict said, "you've asked a very fine question. I hope you find your answer."

With that she dropped the other hand from behind her ear, smiled again, and hurried away, short legs carrying wide shoulders off and leaving Lily grinning in the churchy darkness.

Okay, wow, was all Lily could think.

As she again tuned in to the organ and the soft polishing of the cleaning man's rag, she wasn't sure the conversation had really happened.

That was so strange, she thought—yet as Lily headed for the door before anything *else* weird happened, she realized she didn't feel weird at all. In fact, she felt a little better—like maybe she could go back and deal with Tessa without stuffing that sock in her mouth.

The old lady, with her deaf ear and shelf of a bosom, stuck in Lily's head—until Lily got to the house. She found Tessa in their room, lying on one of the beds—which looked only slightly less lumpy than the couch in the living room—with her feet on the wall, glaring at the ceiling. Lily knew that any minute now she would probably start banging her heels and maybe even doing that yelling thing she'd done back when she first came to live at their house. She hadn't done it in a while, and Lily wasn't ready for her to start it back up, especially not now that they were sharing the same ten-by-ten-foot square of living space. This, she knew, was going to have to be handled carefully.

"So you wanna go home too, huh?" Lily said.

Tessa transferred her green-eyed glare from the ceiling to Lily. "No," she said, "I think it's cool here. I just didn't think everybody was going to dump me like the garbage when we got here."

"Oh, get over yourself," Lily said. "We've only been here an hour—give me a break. I'm here now. Let's fix up our room."

Tessa sprang off the bed as if she had springs on her bottom—which was more than Lily could say for the bed itself—and dove for her suitcase.

"What are we gonna put up on the walls?" Tessa asked. "Mom wouldn't let me bring a Jessica Simpson poster."

Thank you, Mom, Lily thought. But she said quickly, "That's okay. We'll think of something."

The first thing she had to think of was how to stake out some private territory in this cell of a room—and she had to think fast, before Tessa had them signed up for a little too much togetherness. She could already see Tessa trying to figure out how to move the beds closer together.

"First we mark our space," Lily said. "I think I brought a roll of masking tape."

"For putting up posters?" Tessa said, black eyebrows lifted.

"No—you'll see."

Within minutes Lily had dug the tape out of the arts and crafts department of one of her suitcases and stuck a strip of it neatly down the exact center of the room. Tessa stared at it.

"What's that for?" she asked.

"That's for when we need space," Lily said. "If you say I need to stay on my own side of the room for a while, I have to respect that, and vice versa."

"When's that gonna be?" Tessa asked.

Soon, Lily thought. But she tested out Tessa's eyes. They looked a little droopy at the corners, but the potential for heel banging was definitely there.

"Like when we're doing our homework," Lily said, "or one of us is trying to sleep or write in her journal or something."

Lily's voice drifted off. Her talking-to-God time was going to feel pretty funky with Tessa on the other side of that tape line bursting to say stuff.

"But the rest of the time it's just our room, right?" Tessa said.

"Well, yeah," Lily said. "Only we don't touch each other's stuff ever without asking."

Tessa looked around at the bare gray-white walls and the naked tops of the dresser and of the small table squished between their beds. "What stuff?" she asked.

"Yeah—I hear you," Lily said. "We'll just have to be creative with whatever we brought."

Tessa shook her head. "I don't do creative. Mom says I get in trouble when I get too creative."

"Not creative like thinking of ways to get out of taking a spelling test. Creative like"—Lily snatched up her set of markers and tossed them at Tessa—"creative like decorating this tape line."

"What are *you* gonna do?"

Lily frowned. She knew her freckles were folding across her forehead. "I'm going to find a basic way to express myself over here. You can do that on your side, and then we can add stuff as we—"

"As we what?"

"Just … later," Lily said. She couldn't bring herself to say, *As we live out the year—the whole year.*

Instead she turned to her first suitcase, pulled out the yellow bandanna she always wore to the Double H Stables, and spread it over the top of the table between the beds.

"That's on both our sides," Tessa said.

"Oh," Lily said. Once Tessa caught on to a rule and bought into it, she was like a bulldog with the thing. Mom said it was due to lack of structure and security in her old life.

"You want me to fold it in half?" Lily asked.

"Nah," Tessa said. "I like horses too."

Just like you like everything else I like, Lily thought. It was going to be a long year if she didn't lay some more ground rules.

I'm going to be as nice to her as I can when I'm with her, she decided as she continued to haul things out of her suitcases, *but I don't have to be with her all the time. I'm gonna have to find my own thing.*

But as she was taping her collection of pictures of her with her Girlz on the wall above her bed, her heart started to take another dive.

How am I gonna find my own thing all by myself? she thought. *I've always found myself with them—or with some friends anyway.*

She pressed the picture of herself with her cabinmates at camp, taken just a couple of weeks ago, onto the wall and swallowed the lump in her throat. *I never did it alone.*

That, she thought, as she stacked her old and new journals and her new scrapbook into an old laundry basket she found in the closet, *was the whole question. What am I doing here, when I had everything I needed back home?*

And why is that the "right" question? Old Mrs. Benedict didn't know the half of it.

By the time Tessa finished coloring streamerlike hot pink and chartreuse lines on the masking tape and was busy rooting through her luggage, trying to find something to copy Lily's border of ribbons hanging from the ceiling to form a sort of curtain around her bed, Lily had her side looking at least more . . . colorful.

In addition to the ceiling thing, which she considered a stroke of genius, she'd stuffed some of her favorite T-shirts with tights and tied them into throw pillows to brighten up the — of course — beige bedspread. Then she had made a chain of her going-away and birthday cards and notes from people like Mr. Miniver and garlanded it from the corner of the ceiling to the midpoint above the dresser — her half.

Tessa was muttering to herself as she tried to find the stuff to duplicate the whole look on her side, when Mom tapped on the door and poked her head in. Her brown eyes widened.

"Wow," she said.

"You like it?" Lily asked. She was feeling pretty proud of her sweet self. There was a glimmer of hope that this place was not going to get her down after all.

"Wow," Mom said again. "It's like one of the more interesting episodes of *Trading Spaces.*"

"Is that good?" Tessa asked. She shot Mom a sideways look. "I never get to see it. You won't let me stay up that late."

"Don't worry about it, hon," Mom said. "I don't think we'll get it on this TV anyway. What's happening over here?"

She was looking at the two pieces of knotty string that hung from the ceiling on either side of Tessa's bed, and the collection of rolled-up socks lined up against the pillow.

"I'm expressing myself," Tessa said.

"Must be exhausting," Mom said. Her lips twitched the way they did instead of actually smiling. Lily figured she must have enjoyed her alone time.

"Why don't you take a break?" Mom suggested. "Dad says he's taking us to dinner."

Joe stuck his head in the doorway. "Do we have a car yet?"

"No—we'll walk," Mom said.

Joe looked as if he'd been told he had to have a leg amputated. *"Walk?"*

"We won't try to run you into the ground the first night," Mom said. "Give us time."

Tessa was already jamming on her shoes. Lily, on the other hand, was a little sorry to have to leave the room. It was looking like home and that felt good.

Feeling as if she were leaving New Jersey all over again, Lily followed them to the sidewalk out front, where Dad was swinging an umbrella and grinning like a little kid about to burst into Toys R' Us.

"Are you ready for your first look at Oxford?" he asked.

"I've been ready all day!" Tessa said. "I thought I was gonna spend the whole year in the house."

Lily looked at Joe, and they rolled their eyes at the same time. Then Lily quickly looked away. *This is bad if I'm starting to act like him,* she thought.

Mom linked her arm into Dad's—something Lily had never seen her do—and they strolled on ahead, with Dad tossing out pieces of information as the kids followed.

Tessa didn't actually follow for long. She danced ahead and walked backward and nearly ran down several English people with dogs on leashes. It made Lily miss Otto. Joe slunk just behind Mom and Dad, hands jammed into the pockets of the biggest pants he could get away with wearing.

Lily hung back, only half listening to what Dad was saying. It was hard to absorb it all. Everything was so different from Burlington.

"We're now on St. Giles," Dad called back. "This will take us into the *heart* of Oxford, where you'll want to spend most of your time."

Lily saw the street lined with shops and dark-looking restaurants with signs that read "Pub" after their names. What looked to her like a drugstore had a sign that said, "Chemist."

"Most of the buildings you'll see belong to the university and its twenty-nine colleges," Dad said. "Without Oxford *University,* there would probably be no Oxford *town."*

Lily saw damp stone buildings, some with plates that had dates like 1495 and 1610. Most of them looked out sternly at her, as if she couldn't possibly be smart enough to be looking back. It definitely didn't look like Princeton, where Dad taught.

"I don't see any university," Joe said.

"It's spread out all over the city," Dad said, waving his hand as if he himself had planned the whole thing. "Now, the *heart* of the heart of Oxford—they call it the Golden Heart of Oxford—is this series of buildings we're coming up on that reaches from the eastern end of Broad Street down Catte Street to the High Street."

Lily stopped listening and watched almost in a daze as they passed what looked like arch after arch, tower after tower, cream-colored stone wall after cream-colored stone wall of college chapels and dining halls and libraries. There were glimpses of green and gardens as they passed closed gates, but it was all a blur, and it was getting more confusing by the minute.

"It's quite easy to get around," Dad said, already sounding English. "The basic plan of the city is more or less square, divided into four quarters by two main arteries."

"Like blood?" Tessa asked.

"No, like streets, lame-o," Joe said.

Mom shot him a look.

"The east-west is the High Street," Dad said, as if Joe weren't being a jerk, "and the north-south is the line of St. Aldates and the Cornmarket. Those two streets cross—right there—at Carfax. See how simple it is?" He pointed up at a square white tower with a castlelike top. "This tower is at the exact center of ancient Oxford. We'll go up there one day. You can see all of Oxford from there."

Lily looked away from the tower and around at the intersection. The swirl of double-decked red buses and beeping horns and cars all going the wrong direction made her feel almost panicky. *I couldn't find my way around here if I were a bloodhound!* she thought. It was a relief when Dad stepped into a restaurant and out of the confusion. She was glad he'd picked a place with big windows, instead of one of those dark holes that looked as if they'd never let a person out.

And at least she knew what fish and chips were; she ordered them because they were the only thing she recognized on the menu. She wasn't ready to take a chance on shepherd's pie or bangers and mash—whatever they were.

"These don't look like potato chips," Tessa said, holding up a French fry and talking in her usual ball field voice.

Lily didn't check to see if anybody was staring. She already knew they were.

Mom and Dad tried dipping the fries — chips — into vinegar, the way everybody else seemed to be doing it. And Tessa did too, though she made a face and ran for the restroom — the "loo," the waitress told her — to spit it out. Joe asked for ketchup. Lily passed on the fries.

The air was cool and bluish as they walked home, Dad and Mom now holding hands. Something was making them act weird, Joe commented to Lily, and then went back to his sulking. Once again Lily hung back, trying to wrap some thoughts around the place.

Merton College, Exeter College, Queen's College, NEW College, founded in 1379 — what's up with that? I'll never remember all this stuff. Dad's eating it up. Tessa thinks everything rocks. How come I don't feel like that? Everybody thought I would. Maybe it will be better in London, which they said is supposed to be my place.

She stopped abruptly. The street was suddenly quiet — as in Tessa-not-talking quiet.

Lily whipped her head around but her family was nowhere in sight.

"They went that way," said a voice.

It came from the front step of a house — actually what looked like several houses hooked together. And it came out of the mouth of a girl with very blonde hair and very long teenaged legs.

"That was your family, was it?" the girl asked.

"I guess," Lily said.

"You don't know your own family, then?"

"I mean, was it a man, a woman, a boy about eleven?"

The girl was nodding. "And a child who never stops raving on?"

Lily nodded too. "You say they went that way?"

"Yes," said the girl. "But I don't think you need them right now." She patted the step next to her. "I think you need me."

Chapter 4

L ily looked from the girl to the street and back again.

"They've got you on a lead, then?" the girl said to Lily.

"A what?" Lily asked.

"A lead like when you take your dogs on walkies."

"Oh—a leash!" Lily said. She craned her neck for sight of Mom and Dad. "No, I just don't know where I'm going. I'm from—"

"Oh, I know. You're that American family that's just moved into Shirty Sheggs's house."

"His first name is Shirty?" Lily said.

The blonde girl shook her head of short spiky hair. She had enormous pale blue eyes that rolled at Lily. "*I* named him that," she said. "*Shirty* means you're dull and come on all pompous—like you know everything except how to act 'round people."

"Oh," Lily said.

"You could learn a lot from me." The girl patted the step again.

Lily looked up the street again, just in time to see Tessa charging around the curve.

"I can't," she said. "Here comes my sister to get me."

The eyes rolled yet again. "You'd better go on, then. That child would drive me mad."

"Thanks for all the information," Lily said as she edged away.

"Pop 'round anytime," the girl said. "Looks as if you're going to need it. What's your name, by the way?"

"Lily. Lily Robbins."

"Kimble. Kimble Kew. And don't laugh or I'll have to duff you up."

Lily had no idea what that meant but she had no desire to laugh anyway. She just wanted to get to Tessa before she started asking the girl a thousand questions—probably starting with, "How come you're wearing all black?" "Is that the real color of your hair?" and "How do you get it to stick up like that?"

She gave Kimble a wave and practically ran toward Tessa, who met her sucking air like Mom's vacuum cleaner.

"Where'd you go?" Tessa asked.

"I was just talking to someone," Lily said.

"Who?"

"Just some girl who said hi."

"Oh—then she's our neighbor."

They rounded the curve, turned left, and there was their house.

"We could walk there so easily," Tessa said.

I could, Lily thought. *You would drive her mad.*

Feeling slightly smug that she'd learned an English term, Lily flung her arm around Tessa's shoulder.

"Do you want to have a contest?" she asked. "See which one of us can make Joe laugh first?"

"What do I get when I win?" Tessa asked.

"What do you mean, when you win? How about if?"

"You won't win, Lily. You're not funny. I am. What's the prize?"

"You're a bit shirty, aren't you?" Lily said.

"I'm what?"

"Whoever gets Joe to laugh first gets—"

"Chips! Those things are good."

"Okay—we'll go on a walkie and you'll buy me chips."

"Go on a what?"

32

Lily just grinned. Knowing Kimble was going to come in handy.

But it was a whole week before Lily saw the spiky blonde again. There was a lot to do to get settled, like learning where the stores were, and going to Sainsbury's practically every day because the refrigerator was so small, and buying meat that hung from hooks in the Covered Market.

"I can't eat this chicken," Tessa said one night. "I saw its eyes today. It was looking at me."

"It was dead," Joe said.

So far neither Lily nor Tessa had won the contest.

Dad had set up the computer in the dining room, and the family logged on to the Internet. It was almost like being back in Jersey, getting emails from the Girlz—all except Kresha, who didn't have a computer at home. It was the "almost" part that made Lily sad.

Reni wrote,

I so cannot believe you aren't here for eighth grade. It's a huge bummer without you. We have Mrs. Reinhold for English again, and she's way cooler this year. It's like she doesn't have to train us now, so we get to do more fun stuff.

Lily was glad Reni didn't say what the fun stuff was. She wasn't sure she could handle knowing what she was missing. Suzy told her all about how Deputy Dog, the school cop, had already busted Ashley and Chelsea for chasing a boy down the stairs. Lily couldn't help hoping it wasn't Shad. Suzy didn't say.

Zooey went on and on about the new clothes she'd gotten for school and how she hoped Lily would get to dress like the girls in England—and how was that anyway? Could Lily send pictures over the Internet? Wouldn't it be cool, she said, to get pictures from thousands of miles away? It was the thousands of miles that got to Lily.

The only emails that didn't make her sad were Mudda's. First of all, it was hilarious to picture little gray-helmeted Mudda hunched over her brand-new computer. She'd never even used one before Dad bought it for her and showed her how to log on to the Internet.

She wrote,

> I'm only doing this so I can keep you children straight. I vowed I would never use one of these things, and here I am. The things you do to make sure your family doesn't fall off the end of the earth. Lily, watch your father. He tends to drift.

Another day she wrote,

> Lilianna, every day I want you to write to me and tell me the best part of the day — the one new thing you've learned about England in the last twenty-four hours that you know you will know forever.

The first day, Lily wrote back,

> I know what it means to be shirty — and that they call leashes "leads."

It gave her a great deal of satisfaction that Mudda had to write back and ask what "shirty" meant.

But other things weren't so satisfying. As college students began to filter into Oxford for the first term, sporting backpacks, Lily felt herself wishing more and more that she were toting her own pack to Cedar Hills Middle School. Mom hadn't started homeschooling them yet. She planned to start when the kids there in Oxford began. Joe begrudgingly grunted that that was cool. Tessa went mad over it.

"You can *never* start school and that would be okay with me," Tessa said. "I hate to learn."

"That is a big fat lie," Mom said, mouth twitching. "Anybody who asks as many questions as you do couldn't possibly hate to learn."

"That's different," Tessa said. "That's stuff I *want* to know."

34

And want to know she did. Every afternoon, when Dad came back from Magdelan College — which he told them was pronounced "Maudlin," as if it rhymed with "dawdlin' " — he took the three kids, and sometimes Mom, out for a walk around Oxford to explain more things to them. Tessa was always right at his elbow, firing questions at him faster than he could possibly answer them, like, "Why are all the phone booths red?" and "How come they call them 'crisps' instead of potato chips?" and "How come they call that place Radcliffe Camera when it doesn't look anything *like* a camera?"

Dad did manage to get out his answer to that last one, telling her it was the other center of the city, besides Carmax, and that it was the main reading room of the university library, and one of the few grand domes in England, next to St. Paul's Cathedral in London. But Tessa quickly lost interest. She went on to interrogate him about why they called some of the crosswalks "humped zebra crossings."

"I don't see any zebras," she said. "Much less ones with humps."

By about the fourth day Dad was beginning to look stressed, and Lily felt a little sorry for him.

"You have to take turns," Lily said to Tessa. "You can't hog Dad."

Tessa snorted loudly in a piglike fashion, but she gave in and instead became bent on making faces at Joe. Lily wasn't sure if it was in hopes of winning the contest or getting herself popped one.

That day Dad was showing them around Magdelan, the college where he was a Fellow, and where C. S. Lewis, the man he studied, had also been a Fellow — whatever that actually was — starting back in 1925. As they walked around, Dad got that dreamy look his face always took on when he was talking about his work. His blue-like-Lily's eyes went mistily far away, and he looked so much like a boy having a daydream that it was easy to forget his red hair was starting to fade into gray.

"This college was founded in 1458," he told Lily. "Before Columbus even discovered the New World."

"I thought *we* had old stuff in Burlington," Lily said.

Dad pointed to a tower, which he described as "graceful." "It took seventeen years to build that tower," he said. "And every May 1, the bridge there is crowded early in the morning when from the top of the tower, the choir heralds the spring with a Latin hymn."

Behind them Joe yawned loudly.

Dad led them through the gateway into what he told them was St. John's Quad. It was a grassy space surrounded on four sides by the front wall, the Founder's Tower, the Muniment Tower, and the chapel, which had a pulpit on the outside where Dad said once a year a sermon was still preached.

They peeked into the chapel and saw, above the altar, a painting of Christ carrying the cross.

"Hey, there's Jesus!" Tessa called out.

"Let's get her out of here, Dad," Lily whispered.

They hurried through the cloisters, as Dad called them—arched outside walkways on the sides of the buildings, one of which led to a steep staircase that went up to the silent main hall. Even Tessa shut up for a minute when they looked in there. It had polished paneled walls and pictures of the college through the ages.

Dad wasn't taking any chances with Tessa, however, and he herded them out to the grounds.

"Its setting is the most magnificent part of Magdelan," Dad said to Lily as Tessa ran off and Joe followed at an I-don't-care saunter. "See, there's the river—it's the Thames but here they call it the Isis—and look this way."

Lily followed his hand as it wafted toward an endless green meadow against a background of hills, all lined with trees. She could see Tessa and Joe chasing a deer.

"There has been a herd of deer in this grove for two hundred and fifty years," Dad said in a whisper. He sounded as if he were praying. "They say they are magnificent in the winter if it should snow."

Lily looked around at the grass, still so green in the early fall, and she felt as if winter were a thousand years away—as many years as there were miles between here and home. The lump in her throat got too big to swallow. She felt Dad's arm around her shoulders.

"Oh, Lilliputian," he said. "I know you're homesick."

That opened the tear faucet and Lily couldn't turn it off. "I'm sorry," she said. "I know how excited you were about bringing us here, and I was too about coming—only I miss my friends."

"You're going to make new friends."

She forced herself not to shake her head and pretended instead to have to snuff up her nose.

"This is the difficult part, though," Dad said, "before you find companions. I can only tell you what I do in these situations."

Lily was sure her father's advice on making friends wasn't going to be much help. His idea of a friend seemed to be somebody to talk to about stuff nobody else understood. But since no one else seemed to be offering any help in this department, she nodded at him.

"What?" she asked.

"I take that opportunity to make friends with myself," he said. "God is here too. Explore the city and find out where you fit in. Take your journal and write in it. Look for the things that make you happy." He gave her shoulders a squeeze. "And unexpectedly, a friend will appear, and you'll be a more interesting, more real person to fall right into a friendship with that person."

Lily frowned across the meadow at the squealing Tessa. How she was supposed to do all that with her kid sister squalling in her ear was about as clear as algebra.

Dad chuckled. "Is she driving you nuts?"

"She's driving me *mad!* I love her, Dad, but—"

"Say no more. We'll make sure you have plenty of alone time."

It was something, Lily decided. And Dad was true to his word. Mom got to work on it and performed a miracle. She found Tessa and Joe a soccer team—football, as they call it in Britain. They both came back the first day gritting their teeth.

"They're, like, way ahead of us," Joe said to Mom.

"No, they're not!" Tessa said. "Get the ball—we're practicing."

Lily exchanged smiles with Mom as Joe and Tessa bounded out the back door. *This,* Lily thought, *just might work out.*

But as she ventured out her first day by herself, Lily had second thoughts. For openers, she was nervous about getting lost—even if the center of Oxford was just around the corner. She'd been out every day with Dad, but she wouldn't have been able to tell the Radcliffe Camera from the Carmax if her email account had depended on it.

She decided to go over to the church first. That was familiar. And if she ran into Mrs. Benedict, at least it was somebody to talk to. Besides, she felt a strong tug drawing her into the church again. When she entered, all was still. Lily slipped just as silently into a chair in the back and gazed up at the scenes behind the altar.

Mrs. Benedict said God was definitely here, she thought. *I hope she's right. I need him to tell me why I have to be here.*

"Lily, my dear," said a crackly voice near her elbow. "Welcome."

Lily jumped. *Does this woman live here?* she wondered.

"I didn't mean to startle you," Mrs. Benedict said. "May I join you?"

"Sure," Lily said. She slid over to give the old woman room next to her. "I don't know what you're joining, though — I mean, I don't know what I'm doing. I mostly just came in here because I was afraid that if I went anywhere else, I'd get lost."

She knew she was "raving on," as Kimble had put it, but Mrs. Benedict nodded and cupped her hand around her ear as if Lily were making perfect sense.

"Flossed?" she said.

"No," Lily said. "Lost."

"Of course. I've lit a candle for you." Mrs. Benedict nodded toward a light that flickered in a row with some others.

"Is this a Catholic church?" Lily asked.

"No, this is the Church of England. It's an Anglican Church, like your Episcopal Church in the U.S."

"Isn't that *like* Catholic?" Lily asked.

"Only in that we both use beautiful ceremony in our worship. But this church is very Protestant indeed." Her eyes twinkled at Lily. "Don't let on to anyone that I told you."

"Okay," Lily said.

"Now then — don't be afraid to get lost."

Lily felt her eyes widening. Now who wasn't making sense?

"The journey to finding yourself begins with losing your way," the old woman said. "Then you must simply ask the right question, and that you've already done." She nodded, smiling her cobweb of lines into her face. "It seems to me you've got a good start, my dear."

"But I already know myself," Lily started to say—and then she stopped. Dad had said something like that too. Why didn't anybody believe that she already *knew* who she was? She was Lily Robbins, leader of the Girlz Only Club!

"I'll leave you to it, then," Mrs. Benedict said, getting up.

Lily was afraid she'd hurt her feelings.

"Thank you for the advice, Mrs. Benedict," she said.

The old lady laughed, startling the quiet church into echoes. "I'm not Mrs. Benedict," she said. "I'm Sister Benedict."

"Oh—you mean like a nun?" Lily said.

"Exactly like a nun—an Anglican nun," the old woman said. She started to go again, and then she stopped to look over her shoulder. Her nose pointed down at Lily like a friendly, teasing, marbled finger.

"And that wasn't advice I gave you, Lily, my dear," she said. "That was the truth."

Chapter 5

Lily wasn't sure if what Sister Benedict had said was really true or not. But she did email Mudda that night.

I met this old lady — a nun with a huge lumpy nose and a laugh like she's five. She says the journey to finding myself begins when I lose my way. I didn't even know I was supposed to "find myself." I just want to know what I'm doing here, and she just keeps saying that's the right question. I don't know if it's the most important thing that happened today, but it's the most confusing.

The next day Mudda responded,

She sounds like a wonderful old crone. Spend time with her. Listen to her. And in addition to finding the best part of each day, I want you to ask her one very important question each day. I suspect this Benedict woman can answer them.

So Lily decided to take Sister Benedict's "truth." The next day she forced herself not to go to the now familiar church but to walk down the block toward the *"heart* of the heart of Oxford."

If I get lost, she tried to convince herself, *I'm just finding my way.* She headed down Woodstock Road—head up, eyes straight ahead. *Wherever this street takes me, that's where I'm going.*

It sounded kind of adventurous. Reni would think this was cool. Suzy and Zooey, of course, would be freaking out. And Kresha would be right there beside her. She wasn't afraid of much of anything. The sadness of thinking about her Girlz weighed on Lily as if someone were pressing down on her head. She walked faster.

"Is somebody chasing you, then?" said a voice.

Lily looked around at the doorway to the chemist's. Kimble was standing there, tucking a package into her tiny shoulder bag as she observed Lily.

"Where is that gobby sister of yours?"

Lily stopped. "Gobby?"

"She's got a bit of a big mouth on her—in more ways than one."

Kimble stepped out onto the sidewalk and began to walk as if Lily had just invited her along. For a second Lily wondered if this was cheating, but her palms stopped sweating. Cheating or not, it was definitely easier having somebody beside her.

"Where are you off to?" Kimble asked.

"I don't know," Lily said. "I'm just out for a walkie."

Kimble gave her a long look with her huge pale blue eyes. They looked even bigger today because her blonde hair was pushed straight back.

"You're a quick study, then, aren't you?" she said.

"You mean I learn fast?" Lily said.

Kimble nodded. "That's good. Otherwise, they'll eat you up at school."

"I'm not going to school—I mean, my mom's homeschooling us."

"Lucky dog," Kimble said. "I hate school."

"Don't you have friends?"

"Oh—I like the friends. I just hate the school."

Lily nodded and continued to watch Kimble out of the corner of her eye as they walked on, Lily almost running to keep up with Kimble's long legs. She was even taller than Lily, so Lily decided she must be at least fifteen—maybe even sixteen. Kimble certainly talked older than thirteen. There was something so serious about her—more like sarcastic. It made Lily feel too young.

"We're going to Boots," Kimble said suddenly.

"We are?" Lily said.

"You said you were just walking—and don't tell anyone our age that or they will think you are completely wet. You've got to be walking somewhere—so we'll go to Boots."

"What's Boots?" Lily asked. "And what's 'wet'?" she added.

"Your education has been sadly neglected," Kimble said. Her voice went slow and patient. "It's a store. They mostly sell cosmetics—lippy."

"You mean lipstick?" Lily said.

Kimble looked her square in the face. "Yes—and you've got a gorgey mouth. You really do need more lipstick."

Lily sucked her lips in. "My mouth is gorgey?"

"Gorgeous. I wish I had a gob like that. My lips are so thin, you could walk the tightrope on them."

Lily didn't have a chance to check out Kimble's lips before she went into higher gear and they took off down a side street Lily didn't catch the name of. It wouldn't have mattered, because they immediately ducked down several more, and a few alleys, weaving in and out of walls and gardens and around trash cans—Kimble called them dustbins—until suddenly they were standing in front of a large, brightly lit store with neon green and pink and orange scarves hanging in the windows.

Everything's either dark and somber or it's garish, Lily thought. She was beginning to like that word. She wondered if Kimble ever used it.

There was no time to ask that either, because Kimble had already pushed through the glass doors and was making a beeline for the cosmetics section. By the time Lily caught up with her, she had a bright-red "lip" opened for Lily's inspection.

"Try this first," she said.

"Um ... my parents aren't all that crazy about me wearing makeup," Lily said. "See, I'm just thirteen."

"Who isn't?" Kimble said. "Well no, actually, I'm going to be fourteen in just a few months—but who listens to parents anyway? My mum tells me I can't wear makeup at the very moment that I'm rooting through her bag for a panstick for my spots."

Lily didn't know which part of that to address first. But apparently it didn't matter, because Kimble grabbed her by the chin and smeared Candy Apple Red on her lower lip.

"Do this," she said, pressing her lips together.

"Are you sure we're allowed to—"

"If you're going to stand 'round waiting to find out if you're allowed to do things, you'll never get anything done," Kimble said. "It's better to ask for forgiveness than permission—or something like that."

Lily's head was spinning. Kimble took her by the shoulders and faced her into the mirror. A pair of huge red sofas looked back at her.

"Uh, I don't think so," Lily said.

"Right—it is a bit much. Here, wipe it off and we'll try another."

Kimble snatched a tissue out of a box and dove for Lily's lips.

"You know what?" Lily said—as best she could with Kimble scrubbing at her mouth as if she were the bottom of a pot. "I'm thirsty. Let's get something to drink. I'll buy."

Kimble stopped wiping and looked at her as if she were impressed. "So it's true what they say about Americans."

"What?"

"You're all rich."

"No!" Lily said. "We're not rich!"

"If you have more than a Euro in your pocket, you're rich," Kimble said. "Come on—we'll go to the Hoof." And once again they were off, Lily taking two steps for every one of Kimble's and trying to catch her breath, until they reached a sandwich shop called On the Hoof.

It was like that for the rest of the afternoon. Lily was sure that they were in and out of every shop in Oxford—pawing everything from CDs to skirts so small that Lily wasn't sure they weren't really Ace bandages, to tons of cosmetics that Kimble seemed drawn to.

Still—in the times Lily had half a second to consider it—Kimble wasn't like Chelsea and Ashley who were so into makeup and boys. Kimble also seemed interested in Lily herself.

Interested? Lily thought at one point when Kimble was shoving her into a bright blue vinyl jacket. *She wants to do a total makeover on me!*

But it was fun—in a lopsided, wild kind of way. Definitely different from Lily's usual outings with the Girlz, during which *she* was the one calling the shots. As they clipped back toward Lily's street, munching on McVities candy bars, which Kimble had said was the only kind to eat, Lily decided being the follower was good for a change.

"Okay," she said. "So now I know about lips and Boots and McVities—and not to tell anybody I go for walks."

"It's a start," Kimble said. "But there's tons more I have to teach you."

"Why?" Lily asked. "I mean, don't get me wrong, I appreciate it—I'd be so wet if I didn't know this stuff—but how come you're doing it?" She felt her eyes narrowing. "Did my mom put you up to this?"

"I've never met your mum." Kimble shoved the rest of her candy bar into her mouth and licked her fingers, bright red nails slipping in and out of her mouth like flashing pieces of confetti. "That's another thing about you Americans."

"What?"

"You just say whatever comes into your heads."

"Don't you?" Lily asked.

Kimble smiled—Lily realized it was the first time she'd seen her do it. "I suppose I do like to get to the nub of things. But not everyone 'round here does. Most people are actually rather buttoned up."

Lily nodded in fascination.

Kimble stopped at the corner. "Well then, I suppose I'll be going. Will you be out"—she whispered—"walking tomorrow?"

"Oh no," Lily said. "I wouldn't want people to think I was wet."

Kimble nodded her approval. "Good. Why don't you come 'round about the same time, and we'll go down to the river and see if there are any boys we fancy. They should be out punting."

Lily nodded uncertainly.

"Uh-oh," Kimble said. "Your parents aren't crazy about you seeing boys, either, are they?"

"It's never come up," Lily said. "I mean, I never really 'liked' a boy—except Shad—but he doesn't exactly count, because I don't know if I *like* him like him or just like him."

"You don't have to like them," Kimble said. "We're just going to look at them. Tomorrow then?"

"Sure," Lily said as Kimble disappeared around the corner. The rest of the way home, Lily wondered what she was going to tell Mudda was the most important part of *this* day.

But she didn't get straight to the computer, because Dad met her in the dark front hallway, grinning as if they'd just won the lottery.

"Lilliputian! Come in here—there's someone I want you to meet."

"Who?" Lily whispered.

"A friend for you," Dad said. And before Lily could even get the uneasy feeling in the pit of her stomach which a statement like *that* usually brought on, Dad was pulling her into the living room. Lily stopped in the doorway and stared as a boy of about thirteen stood up from the lumpy couch and stared back from the top of a long, pointy nose.

"Lily, this is Ingram," Dad said. "Ingram, my daughter Lily."

All Ingram said then was, "How do you do?" But it was enough for Lily to know that poor Ingram was definitely—wet.

Chapter 6

It wasn't that Ingram was ugly or anything—he really wasn't. He had light strawberry blond hair parted in the middle and cut short around the sides, and his eyes were very blue. Even the few pimples on his chin—spots, Kimble had called them—weren't any worse than on any other thirteen-year-old boy she'd ever seen. Shad had those. It wasn't even the pointy nose or the skinniness.

No, it was definitely the fact that Ingram was madly blinking at her out of contact lenses he'd obviously just gotten and wasn't used to. And there was the fact that he'd just said, "How do you do?" Nobody thirteen years old says, "How do you do?"

"I'm fine, I guess," Lily said.

He looked at her as if she were speaking French.

Then neither of them said anything. Lily looked at her father with, *Dad why are you doing this to me!* in her eyes. He seemed to miss that completely.

"Ingram's father is at Magdelan," Dad said. "We got to talking and discovered we had kids the same age—and with a lot in common."

Like what? Lily thought. *We're both human beings?*

Dad clapped his hands together. "Well, I guess you two will want to get acquainted."

Guess again! Lily wanted to scream.

But Dad was already on his way out of the room. "I'll see what your mother has for snacks," he said over his shoulder and then disappeared down the hallway.

Lily turned back to Ingram and hoped she didn't look as completely clueless as she felt right now. Ingram was still blinking at her.

"So—you don't have to stand up," Lily said. "Of course, that's a pretty bad couch. You could try one of the chairs."

Lily herself flopped down on the hard floor. She'd figured out that Ingram was at least two inches shorter than she was, which made her feel even more like a geek than she already did, and that was considerable.

Ingram sat stiffly on one of the leather chairs and eased back into it as if he were afraid it was going to bite him. And then he blinked.

They stared at each other for a second and then both looked at the ceiling, the floor, and the lumpy couch until Lily couldn't stand it any longer.

"So—," she said, "do you know Kimble Kew?"

"No," Ingram said. "Should I?"

He sounded so proper, Lily wondered if she should curtsy or something. As it was, she made sure her skirt was covering her knees.

"She's our age," Lily said. "I thought maybe you went to school together."

"I go to a boys' school," Ingram said. "I don't know many girls, actually."

"Oh," Lily said. "Well, I'm a girl and now you know me—sort of."

She wanted to cover her face with her hands—or better yet, jump out the window. As it was, she squeezed her eyes shut for a second and then tried again.

"Do you *want* to know any girls?" she asked. "I mean—are you mad at your dad for making you come over here?"

"There was no force involved," Ingram said. "I wanted to come. I was told you had an interest in literature and history and so on."

He stopped blinking for a second and looked at Lily as if he were sure he'd been given the wrong information.

47

"Oh!" Lily said. "I do … I mean, I am … I like that stuff."

Ingram went back to blinking doubtfully at the ceiling. Lily felt as if she had to say something at least halfway intelligent. This boy was starting to annoy her, trying to act all superior.

"Well, so I guess you know a lot about Oxford, then," she said.

Ingram looked at her. "I know everything."

"Everything?" Lily said. "All those dates and … things?"

"Ask me anything."

Lily couldn't even think of a question. But Ingram's eyes had suddenly taken on a bit of a gleam, and she felt herself sitting up straighter. He really was shirty.

"Okay," Lily said. "Um—what's the oldest building in Oxford?" Dad had just told her the day before.

"Saxon Tower of St. Michael's in the Cornmarket," Ingram said without so much as a blink.

"What was the first steeple built in England?"

"Christ Church Cathedral, right here in Oxford. See here—these questions are too *easy.*"

"These are the hardest ones I can think of!" Lily said. "I can't ask questions if I don't know anything!"

She could feel her face going blotchy, though she was sure this kid wouldn't notice. But she did rearrange herself a little on the floor so she wouldn't *look* as ticked off as she was getting.

"Yes, well, right," Ingram said calmly. "I suppose that's what your father wants me to do, then—show you around and educate you."

"I'm going to be homeschooled," Lily said, voice cool.

"No, I mean learn the way I've done," Ingram said. He sat upright in the chair and rubbed his hands together as if he were in full charge. It was like watching some miniature professor at work. "You've got to climb 'round in the spires and walk the halls and such. It's the only way to learn it, really." He looked down his nose at Lily. "That is, if you're really willing to learn."

"Of course I'm willing," Lily said. "I'm a serious student."

She'd never actually put it exactly that way before, but she had to say something to this conceited little creep.

"Are you, now?" Ingram said.

"Yes!"

"Yes, well, right—it's just that I never saw a serious student wear quite so much lip, if you get my meaning."

Lily refused to put her hand up to her mouth or to explain. She merely stared Ingram down and said, "Do you have a problem with that?"

"I just don't want to waste my time on someone who isn't really interested."

"What *time?*" Lily asked.

"The time it's going to take to teach you everything. I have crew most afternoons, polo some days, and then of course my studies. It gets more difficult in third form, you know."

Lily didn't know but she nodded. *Where,* she wondered, *is this going?*

Ingram seemed to be calculating some major math problem in his head. Finally he said, "I suppose Tuesdays and Thursdays after four I could take you 'round. Shall we start tomorrow?"

Before Lily could answer, Dad breezed back in with a plate of cookies that were oozing jelly.

"I got the package away from Tessa," he said. "Mom picked them up at the store and Tessa thinks they're better than Oreos."

"Jammy Dodgers," Ingram said, eyeing them. "I rather fancy them myself. But I have to go."

"Take some for the road," Dad said, sliding the plate toward him.

Ingram caught several as they slipped into the air, and stuffed them into his pocket. Then he turned to Lily and said, "I'll pop 'round about four tomorrow, then. It was nice to meet you."

"Okay," Lily said faintly.

She stood in the doorway as Dad escorted Ingram out.

"Gee!" Dad said as the door closed behind him. "That went well!"

"Yeah," Lily said between gritted teeth. "Great."

Later Lily wrote to Mudda,

I met two people today, and I guess they're each going to show me different sides of Oxford — sort of.

Mudda wrote back the next morning,

> Good. And while you're out, remember to walk barefoot at least once a day. It's a good way to absorb the culture.

I can see it all now, Lily thought. *Kimble will think I'm wet, and Ingram—who* is *totally wet—will call me "uncivilized" or something.*

And speaking of Kimble and Ingram—she now had a problem. How was she going to run around with Kimble *and* do her thing with Ingram? Not that she really wanted to hang out with Blinking Boy, but it was as if she didn't have a choice. And Dad had looked so proud of himself—as if he'd just fixed her life.

Thanks, Dad, she thought. *But I think you just made it worse.*

Lily decided the only way to work it out was to meet Kimble and just be back by four to do whatever it was she had to do with Ingram—for as short a time as possible. Maybe if she acted as if she were completely bored with Oxford history, he wouldn't want to take her around again. London was sounding better all the time—although he probably had that whole city memorized too.

Lily didn't tell her mom about that part of her plan. When she explained the next day how she was going to handle things time-wise, though, Mom frowned.

"That means you're gone all afternoon. I know we promised you that you wouldn't have to be with Tessa every minute, but she needs a little Lily time too, just until she makes some friends."

"Isn't she making friends at soccer—football—whatever it is?"

Mom's mouth twitched. "I don't know about friends—competitors maybe. I'm not sure all those bruises she's coming home with are accidental." She bounced her ponytail as she turned around. "Can you take Tessa with you when you and your friend—what's her name, Kimberly—go out?"

"Kimble," Lily said. "And Mom, do I have to? Tessa just jacks her jaws the whole time and that'll totally turn Kimble off. She won't even want to hang out with me."

"I'll tell Tessa to button it up," Mom said. "I'll threaten her with no Jammy Dodgers if she acts up."

"Mo-om."

"Li-il." Mom turned back around to face Lily, hands planted behind her on the kitchen counter. "This is a big adjustment for all of us, and no matter how much of a front Tessa puts up, she's as scared as anybody. You are her anchor. I would appreciate it if you'd take a little time with her. Just for now."

Mom didn't say it was an order. She was actually being pretty cool about it, saying she would "appreciate it," rather than that Lily had better do it or else. So Lily nodded, popped a Jammy Dodger into her mouth, and went up to find Tessa.

"I smell cookies," Tessa said when Lily appeared in the doorway.

"Get your shoes on," Lily said. "We're going out."

"Where?"

"Around. With a friend of mine."

"Your girlfriend or your boyfriend?" Tessa asked.

"Boyfriend?" Lily said. "I don't *have* a boyfriend!"

"What about that kid who was here yesterday?"

"He is *so* not my boyfriend! In fact"—she brought her face close to Tessa's—"don't even mention him to Kimble. Pretend he was never here."

Tessa's green eyes gleamed. "How much is it worth to ya?"

"My entire share of the Jammy Dodgers," Lily said.

"You're on. I love those things."

"You'll like McVities even better. If you don't run your mouth too much while we're with Kimble, I'll buy you one."

Kimble was waiting at the corner when Lily and Tessa got there. Her big blue eyes went quickly from Tessa to Lily.

My mom made me bring her, Lily mouthed to her.

Tessa didn't see. She was studying the spikes in Kimble's hair.

"Okay, so, I gotta ask," Tessa said. "How do you get it to do that?"

Lily groaned inwardly. This was going to be a long afternoon.

But Kimble seemed to assess the situation and have an immediate solution. She squatted in front of Tessa, put her face near Tessa's nose, and said, "Now

51

look here, kid. Your sister and I have some serious business to take care of. If you want to be part of it, you'll keep your lip buttoned and your eyes sharp."

"Sharp for what?" Tessa asked.

"For boys, of course. Your sister and I are going boy looking, and we can't have eyes in the backs of our heads, so we're counting on you to keep up with what's going on behind us."

Tessa looked up at Lily, who merely shrugged.

"Okay," Tessa said. "But I gotta warn you—they're all creeps to me."

"Oh, of course they are," Kimble said. "But they're nice to look at."

"Whatever," Tessa said.

But she fell in behind them, and when Lily peeked over her shoulder, Tessa had her head going in both directions at once, narrowing her eyes at everything that looked the slightest bit masculine.

"You're a genius," Lily whispered to Kimble.

"I'm brilliant," Kimble said. "Don't forget that."

Then Kimble picked up the pace, so that Tessa had to jog to stay up, and led them to Magdelan.

"This is my dad's college!" Tessa said.

"That's nice," Kimble said, "but we're not going to the college—we're going down here. Try and keep up, would you?"

They made a sharp turn and headed to a grassy area below the bridge.

"They'll be punting on the River Isis today," Kimble said.

"Kicking balls?" Tessa asked. Lily could hear her voice brightening. She was obviously getting tired of boy watching already.

"No, my little ignorant one," Kimble said. "Punting—poling 'round in a punt. Like that."

She pointed toward the water, where a college-age boy was standing in a small rowboat, using a long pole to push the boat along while a brunette sprawled in the bottom of the boat, laughing up at him.

"Did she just call me ignorant?" Tessa asked Lily, eyes going to slits.

"She just meant you didn't know any better—," Lily started to say.

But Tessa abruptly took off for the riverbank, where she stopped, took a long gander at the boat, and then ran back to them, yelling her head off.

"Does she ever speak as if she weren't at a football game?" Kimble asked.

"Never," Lily said. "In fact, sometimes it's worse."

"That *rocks!*" Tessa said when she got to them. "I wanna do that! Can we?"

"I don't happen to own a punt," Kimble said. "Otherwise, of course we could. But remember why we're here."

Tessa's eyes stormed over and Lily cringed, waiting for the thunder. But Tessa's brow suddenly smoothed out and she shrugged.

"Okay," she said. "I better get lookin'."

She turned to dash off. Kimble sat on the grass and patted the spot beside her for Lily.

"Stay where I can see you," Lily called to Tessa. "If you can't see me—"

"I know—'I can't see you,'" Tessa yelled over her shoulder.

"And if we can't *hear* you," Kimble said under her breath, "so much the better." She shook her head at Lily. "There won't be a bloke worth looking at within thirty kilometers with her around."

"Sorry," Lily said. "It won't be forever—just till she makes her own friends."

"I'd better get to work on that then," Kimble said. "Now then, look 'round you, Lily. What do you see?"

Lily leaned back on her elbows and took in the setting. Dad was right—this really was the prettiest part of Oxford.

"There's the bridge...," she began.

"No, no, do you see any masculine young things lurking about?"

"Oh," Lily said. She let her eyes roam. "Well, there's that one in the boat."

"Too old."

"And that one over there, reading the book."

"Too studious. Complete bore."

"Shirty," Lily put in. "And then there's—oh no."

"What?"

Lily sat up and pointed to a tall lanky boy—the one Tessa was leading toward them as she chattered like a chicken.

"What is she doing?" Kimble whispered. "She's bringing him over here!"

She'd barely squeaked out the last word when the boy was standing near their feet, grinning down at them.

"Hello there," he said. "I'm told one of you wants to go punting."

Chapter 7

Lily had the urge to break into hysterical giggles. It was either that or slug Tessa on the spot. Tessa herself was looking pretty smug, as if she'd just brought home an A+ on a spelling test.

"He has a boat!" Tessa said. "And he said he'd take me if one of you would go too."

"I can take you both," Boat Boy said, "but only one at a time, since we'll have the little one along."

"I'm not that little," Tessa said. "I'm just small for my age."

Boat Boy looked at Lily. "Why don't you come along first?"

"Me?" Lily said. "I don't know how to punt!"

"You don't have to," he said. "I'll be doing all the work."

Kimble gave her a nudge in the back. "Go on, Lily. All you have to do is sit on the boat and look gorgey."

"I don't wanna look gorgey," Tessa said. "I want to try doing that pole thing."

"You can help me," Boat Boy said. He stuck out his hand. Lily looked at it blankly.

"He wants to help you up!" Kimble hissed at her.

"Oh," Lily said and then, ignoring his hand, she scrambled to her feet, nearly kicking Kimble in the face and tripping as she stumbled forward.

Boat Boy grabbed her elbow to steady her. "Are you all right, then?" he asked.

"Sure," Lily said.

But her thoughts were screaming at her. *No, you are not all right! You're about to get in a boat with a strange guy who's about five years older than you are! What are Mom and Dad gonna say?*

It was obvious that she shouldn't be doing this. She stopped and pulled her elbow away from Boat Boy.

"Don't be nervous," he said. "I told you, you don't have to do a thing. Only one of us can stand up with the pole at one time anyway."

"But—"

He had taken hold of her elbow again and had her almost to the bank, where Tessa was prancing around by the boat as though she seriously had to go to the bathroom. Lily looked frantically over her shoulder at Kimble, who was staring at her with utter admiration.

Whether it was the sudden rise in Kimble's esteem or the fact that Boat Boy wasn't letting go of her elbow or that if she didn't go, Tessa was probably going to push her into the river, Lily found herself stepping down into the boat. Tessa leaped in, rocking the whole thing until water sloshed over the sides.

"Eager little beaver, eh?" he said.

"Tessa, sit down," Lily said.

"No! I'm gonna help drive—"

"Tes-sa!"

This couldn't possibly get more embarrassing. And then it did. As Lily reached up to tug at the bottom of Tessa's T-shirt, Tessa jerked away—and suddenly disappeared with a splash into the River Isis.

"Tessa!" Lily cried. She tried to scramble up, lurching the boat nearly on its side.

"Hold on, it's not deep," Boat Boy said, grinning down into the water.

"She can't swim!" Lily said.

She managed to get to her feet and jumped over the side into water so cold, it took her breath away. Nearby Tessa was splashing and sputtering, arms flailing wildly as she tried to scream.

"Stop it!" Lily shouted at her. "I'll get you—just let me get you!"

At the sound of Lily's voice, Tessa turned and flung her waving arms around her, pulling them both under the water. Panic surged up in Lily and she had to force herself not to shove Tessa away. Instead she grabbed both of Tessa's wrists, pushed her straight out in front of her, and kicked until they both emerged, sputtering, above the water.

"I've got you!" Lily shouted at her. "Chill! Chill!"

Tessa stopped struggling and started to cry—something Lily had rarely seen her do. Lily took advantage of the moment to turn her around by the shoulders and hold her against her chest, arms pinned down. Lily's legs were already getting tired of treading.

"Here—grab on!" Boat Boy said.

He stuck the pole out and Tessa lunged for it, wrapping herself around it like a fireman. Slowly he pulled Tessa and pole toward him. It obviously wasn't fast enough for Tessa, because the instant she could reach the boat, she lunged and grabbed the side, almost hurling Boat Boy into the water. He managed to get hold of her and pin her down into the bottom of the boat, where he held her with his foot.

"Get off me, you big creep!" she screamed.

"Stop raving on like a madwoman or you'll land us both in the drink!" he shouted back.

Lily waved a hand as her chin dipped once again below the surface. Her legs were beginning to feel like broken rubber bands.

"Hello!" she said.

"Oh—right!" Boat Boy said.

All smoothness was gone now as he pointed his pole out into the water again and let Lily get hold of it. In fact, he looked as if he were sorry he'd ever tried to be Mr. Smooth in the first place.

You and me both, pal, Lily thought as he dragged her toward the boat. *You're lucky I'm about to strangle her or I'd take you out first.*

The only thing good about going home that day, Lily thought later, was that she won the contest. Joe took one look at her bedraggled form coming into the kitchen and collapsed onto the floor, laughing.

But from the looks on her parents' faces, Lily was sure she and Tessa wouldn't be allowed out of the house for chips—or anything else—the rest of the time they were in England. So much for London.

"What puddle did you two fall into?" Mom asked, already coming at them with a towel.

"The river, and it was gross—it was full of swan poop," Tessa said. "Only I didn't fall—Lily pushed me!"

"I did not!"

"Did so. I was gonna do that punting thing and you grabbed my shirt—"

"You wouldn't sit down in the boat—"

"You were in a boat?" Mom said.

"Punting?" Dad said.

"What on earth is punting?" Mom asked.

"It was gonna be cool. This guy was gonna teach me, until Lily messed it up—"

"What guy?" Mom and Dad asked together.

"Oooh—busted," Joe said.

Everyone in the room gave him a withering look that sent him scampering to the table, where he straddled a chair and covered his smirk with his hand. Mom turned back to a shivering Lily.

"Now let me get this straight," Mom said.

With Dad's hand planted firmly over Tessa's mouth until it was her turn to speak, they managed to get the whole thing sorted out. Tessa told all—and made it sound as if Lily and Kimble had actually asked her to fetch them a boy. Although Lily tried to straighten her folks out, their faces were long and disappointed.

"All right, bottom line," Mom said.

Lily winced. Time for the sentencing. She had visions of that room upstairs closing in on her.

"None of you," Dad said, including Joe, "is to get into a vehicle or vessel of any kind without our permission. Understood?"

There were three nods.

"And from now on," Mom said, "we will need to meet your friends before you start spending time with them. We just want to make sure they know what your ground rules are too."

"Of course, it's always up to you to follow our rules, no matter what kind of pressure other people put on you," Dad said.

"I know," Lily said. "I shouldn't have let Tessa drag me into that—"

"Oh, so now it's all *my* fault!" Tessa said.

"Well, you started it—"

"And from now on," Mom broke in, "you will each take responsibility for your own actions."

"Responsibility," Tessa said. She sniffed as if something were rotting in the refrigerator. "That means our punishment for messing up."

Out of the corner of her eye, Lily could see Joe practically licking his chops, but she kept her eyes focused on Dad. *If I believed I was miserable here before,* she thought, *I probably haven't seen anything yet.* Suddenly walking around Oxford was sounding pretty good, now that she wasn't going to get to do it ever again without Mom or Dad along.

"I don't like to think of it as your 'messing up,'" Dad said. "It's a learning experience. What did you learn?"

"That boys are nothin' but trouble," Tessa said.

"Important life lesson," Mom said. Her mouth was twitching.

"And all that other stuff you said, about not goin' in cars and boats, and bringin' our friends home," Tessa added.

"That," Lily said, "and I guess not to hang out with Kimble."

"We didn't say you couldn't hang out with Kimble," Mom said. "We'd just like to meet her. Maybe her parents too."

"Never mind," Lily said. "She's not like the Girlz. You probably wouldn't like her. She has weird hair and she wears makeup."

"Do you like her?" Dad asked.

Lily looked at him in surprise. "She's been really nice to me. She's teaching me how to talk so I won't sound all stupid and wet. She's fun."

"Give us some credit, Lil," Mom said. "We don't judge people by their haircuts. If you really like her and you want to be her friend, bring her over and let us get to know her."

58

"I think you know yourself well enough not to be completely influenced by somebody else," Dad said. "We just want to make sure she's willing to follow our rules when she's with you."

Lily stifled a groan. "You're going to give her a lecture when she comes over here?"

"I promise we'll keep it to under an hour," Mom said dryly. "Why don't you two go upstairs and get cleaned up."

"Oh, that's right, Lilliputian," Dad said, glancing at his watch, "Ingram will be here at four."

Aw, man, Lily thought as she trudged upstairs. *I should have let myself drown in the Isis.*

But fifteen minutes later she was standing on the front steps of her house next to Ingram, with Dad behind her in the doorway saying, "You two kids have a blast."

There was no need for him to explain the ground rules to Ingram, Lily thought. The kid probably had a few of his own. As a matter of fact, he did. Before they'd gone two steps down the sidewalk, Ingram cleared his throat and said, "Yes, well, right."

"Right what?" Lily said. She tried not to sound as if she would gladly snatch him baldheaded if he insulted her.

"Yes, well—I thought we would climb to the top of Carfax Tower and see the entire city so you can have a look at it all together."

"Fine," Lily said.

"Yes, well, right—but they don't allow any carrying on up there, if you get my meaning."

"No, I don't get your meaning," Lily said.

"No tossing things from the tower, that sort of thing."

Lily turned to stare at him. "What gives you the idea that I would do something like that?"

"Yes, well, right."

"Stop saying that!"

Lily stopped dead on the sidewalk to face him. Ingram was blinking furiously. It was the first time Lily had seen him look the way *she* felt around *him* every other minute. She didn't feel sorry for him.

"All right, here it is," Ingram said. "My dad saw you bobbing about in the river this afternoon — you and your sister. He told me Americans tended to go doolally."

"Well, he told you wrong," Lily said. Her face was so stiff, she could barely move her mouth, which she knew was probably a good thing. It was keeping her from saying what she *really* felt like saying — and she'd obviously embarrassed her father enough already. She could just imagine how Dad was going to feel when Ingram's father got in his face in the hall at Magdelan, going on about her dip in the Isis.

"I wouldn't want you to embarrass yourself," Ingram said.

"You don't want me to embarrass *you*, you mean," Lily said. Ingram just blinked. "Don't worry. I won't."

"Good then," Ingram said. "Shall we go?"

"Yes, we shall."

Ingram took off at a brisk clip and Lily matched him step for step. As she marched along, trying not to sound as if she were gasping for her next breath, she left behind her plan to act so bored by Oxford history that Ingram would never want to take her around again.

No way, she told herself. *There is no way I am going to give this little creep the satisfaction of being able to call me a doolally American — whatever that is. No way!*

Chapter 8

For an hour Lily strode around Oxford at Ingram's side, willing herself to keep her head up and her questions intelligent. There wasn't one Ingram couldn't answer, of course.

They climbed first to the top of Carfax Tower, where Ingram said the view of Oxford was "unrivaled." Lily had to admit it was pretty impressive and tried to think of a word that would top *unrivaled*. *Awesome* was the best she could come up with. From there she could see the whole city at once, and it reminded her of a giant sand castle, with all its cream-colored stone buildings built around green squares and with its steeples pointing up from towers decked with columns and statues. It didn't seem real.

"Those steeples are magnificent," Lily said in her best public-speaking voice. Mrs. Reinhold, she knew, would have been proud.

"They're spires, actually," Ingram said. "The poet Matthew Arnold called them 'dreaming spires.'"

In spite of her annoyance at being corrected, Lily liked the dreaming spires part. They did look like something out of a fantasy, each decorated like a wedding cake, with a crownlike top and a tiny cross.

"The University Church of St. Mary the Virgin on the High Street has the best spire," Ingram said, pointing to an especially tall one surrounded at its base with smaller points. "Fifteenth century. It has a bit of baroque—it's quite extraordinary."

"Oh, quite," Lily said. "And that of course is the Radcliffe Camera—and the Bodleian Library. It's terribly plain, actually." She smiled smugly at Ingram.

"Not on the inside," he said. "The vaulting in the Divinity School is rather elaborate."

"Is it, now?" Lily said. She groped for another intelligent question—one she hoped Ingram couldn't answer. She came up with, "How many books do you suppose they have in that library?"

"I don't suppose," Ingram said. "I know. There are two and one half million. Every new book published in Great Britain is placed there. The Radcliffe Camera has six hundred thousand."

"Wow," Lily said. She felt an actual spark of interest. "So many books—so little time."

"You like to read, then?" Ingram said as he headed for the stairs.

"I would rather read than eat."

"And what sort of thing do you read?"

He stopped at the top of the stairs to look at her. The doubt in his blinking eyes snagged at Lily like barbed wire.

"Shakespeare," she said. "Jane Austen. That sort of thing."

"Yes, well, right," Ingram said. "Jane Austen is for girls."

"Well, yeah, hello—I'm a girl," Lily said.

From there they went to the round Sheldonian Theatre, which Ingram told her was a "lavish setting for university ceremonial." As Lily stared through the fence with its stone posts topped with the heads of statues, Ingram informed her that he didn't think she'd ever see the inside of it, since her father was an American Fellow and not really a part of the university.

And he thinks Americans are rude! Lily thought. She gnawed at her lip and followed him to the Old Ashmolean, which he told her was the oldest museum building in the world. They didn't go in. Ingram said he wanted to give her the general tour of the city and then go back another day and work on the specifics. Lily moaned to herself. Another day of being told how inferior she was? Wonderful.

They saw the "Bridge of Sighs," which was a romantic looking bridge that connected two buildings of Hertford College, and Martyrs Memorial, a spire on the ground, rising from steps where chatting, laughing students were gathered in clumps. Ingram explained that it was a nineteenth-century memorial to Archbishop Cranmer and Bishops Ridley and Latimer, who were burned at the stake during Queen Mary's reign.

"So it's new for Oxford," Lily said.

"Yes, well, right," Ingram said. "Now, if it's old that you want—"

"It is," Lily said. "The older the better. I'm very serious about history."

"Yes, well, right," Ingram said. "We'll pop over to St. Michael at the Northgate, then."

On the way, Lily decided to risk sounding stupid and ask Ingram why those people were burned by the queen.

"You don't know?" he said.

"If I knew, I wouldn't have asked," Lily said.

"Yes, well, right." Ingram stopped at a corner to let a double-decker bus go by and gave an elaborate sigh. "All right, well, there was the Church of England, which had broken away from the Roman Catholic Church during the reign of King Henry VIII."

"I heard that was because he wanted a divorce and the pope wouldn't let him," Lily said.

"That's just malicious gossip," Ingram said, as if it had just happened yesterday at Cedar Hills Middle School. "The church itself was already established. Henry merely recognized it as the official religion of England when he wanted his divorce."

"Go on," Lily said. In spite of Ingram's sounding as if her ignorance on the subject were more unbelievable than a UFO sighting, she was getting interested.

"His daughter Mary was Catholic, so of course she went mad when her father did that. When it was her turn to reign, after Henry died and his son Edward died, she reestablished the Catholic Church as the official church and executed all the leaders of the Church of England who wouldn't become Catholic."

"How could she do that?"

Ingram blinked at her. "Because she was the queen. They called her Bloody Mary."

"They should have called her worse than that!"

By now they had reached a square stone tower that looked like something out of a King Arthur movie Lily had once seen. This, she knew, was *way* before Shakespeare's time.

"This is, like, medieval," Lily said.

"It isn't 'like' medieval," Ingram said, eyes blinking faster than ever. "It *is* medieval."

Lily stopped at the foot of the tower and gazed up at its ancient craggy stones and its bare unblinking windows cut in the shape of tablets. It was plain, almost crude, but it seemed to sigh down at Lily as if it were heavy with the burden of the years it had seen. Lily reached out and ran her fingers over the stones. They were cool and unyielding.

"It makes me sad," she murmured.

"It should," Ingram said.

Lily felt herself blotching. She hadn't meant for him to hear that.

"Sad things happened here," he said. "The Bocardo prison was once attached to the church."

"A prison at the church?"

Ingram sighed patiently. "The church, the throne—it was all one and it ruled the country. They tore the prison down in the eighteenth century but it was on this spot. And Archbishop Cranmer was confined here before he was martyred."

"Poor man," Lily said.

"Do you want to see the door to his cell, then?" Ingram asked.

"I thought you said they tore the prison down."

"They kept the door—they have it inside the church. Unfortunately, it's closed right now or you could see it."

Lily felt herself sagging. Just as she'd felt whenever she went into St. Margaret's, she felt something tugging at her, pulling her toward the church. Instead she stood in front of the tower until Ingram began to sigh again, and she imagined the great Thomas Cranmer, whom she'd never heard of until today, waiting inside the prison, ready to die for his faith.

I've been ready to give up a lot of things—like the Girlz or something for a cause we had, Lily thought. *But I wonder if I would ever be willing to die for something.*

The thought made her feel small. And then the shadows began to lengthen and Lily knew it was time to head home. She told Ingram she could find her own way home, but he shook his head.

"That wouldn't be proper," he said.

Lily thought of asking him if he ever did anything that *wasn't* proper, but as they headed for Woodstock Road, she had another, more important question.

"Do you know any other old churches in Oxford?" she asked.

"Do I know my name?" Ingram said. "I know them as well as—"

"Would you take me to some, then?" Lily asked.

Ingram took a long look at her. Lily looked back and forced herself not to blink. She was going to have to look up the word *arrogant* in the dictionary, but she was pretty sure his picture would be next to the definition. If there were other people around to take her, she would definitely be asking them!

"Yes, well, right," Ingram said. "I'll take you to Christ's Church. It's small as cathedrals go, but it has the first steeple ever built in all of England."

"I want to go there," Lily said.

"I want to save that until last, actually. There are others to show you before that. Tomorrow, then—but we'll have to go earlier. Say about two?"

"Uh—okay," Lily said. That would probably work, since she was going to have to have Kimble over before she could go out with her again anyway.

And then, as if by merely thinking of her she could made her appear, Lily saw Kimble herself, lounging in the doorway of the chemist's.

Aw, man! Lily thought. *She's going to see me with Ingram, and she's never going to want to hang out with me again!*

But there was no avoiding her. Kimble had obviously already spotted Lily, and she took the steps all in one long-legged stride, planting herself on the sidewalk in front of them.

"I beg your pardon," Ingram said. His blinking went into overdrive.

"It's okay—I know her," Lily said. "Kimble, this is Ingram."

"How do you do?" Ingram said.

Kimble stared at him for a full ten seconds and then said, "Fine, thank you, and yourself?"

Ingram muttered something and folded his arms across his chest. Kimble turned abruptly to Lily.

"Well then, what did your mum and dad say? Was there a row?"

Lily shifted her eyes at Ingram but Kimble didn't seem to take the hint. She just opened her eyes wider.

"Did they go mad?" she asked.

"No," Lily said through gritted teeth. "I'll tell you all about it later."

"Where are you going now?'

"Home."

"Mind if I come along?"

Lily let her eyes dart to Ingram again but Kimble seemed to have decided he was invisible. She had already fallen into step beside Lily.

"Where have you been?" Kimble asked.

"Oh—just around," Lily said.

Ingram cleared his throat and looked past her at Kimble. "We've been exploring the historical aspects of the city of Oxford," he said. "Lily is a serious student of history."

Lily looked around for a hole to dive into.

"Is she really?" Kimble said. Her voice went into a high pitch and her words came out in sharp little points. "Now, isn't that just marvelous? And I suppose you're her tutor."

"Something like that," Ingram said. His face was going paler than its usual Elmer's Glue white.

"I'm her tutor too, in a manner of speaking."

Lily looked again for that hole.

"One can only imagine what *you* are teaching her," Ingram said.

"And what does one imagine?" Kimble asked.

"Cosmetics, slang, bad habits."

"Right-o!" Kimble said. "All the things she's going to need to survive here."

They were within sight of Lily's house, and Ingram stopped.

"I think I'll go on now," he said. "I'll be 'round at two tomorrow."

"Yeah," Lily said. "See ya."

Ingram gave Kimble one last blinking look and said, "Nice to meet you."

"Charmed, I'm sure," Kimble said.

Then she barely waited until Ingram was out of earshot before she let out a large guffaw that rivaled anything Lily had ever heard from an American.

"Why are you hanging 'round with that perfect whelk?" Kimble asked.

"I know he's a bit shirty—"

"Shirty? He's positively medieval!"

"Yeah, he is—"

"It must be complete aggers for you to be around him. Are your mum and dad forcing you to?"

"Well, kind of, but—"

Kimble put her hand on Lily's shoulder. "You don't fancy him, do you?"

"You mean like him?"

"For heaven's sakes, he's got the longest conk I've ever seen—"

"Conk?"

"Nose. And that fringe. Nobody wears his hair in a fringe anymore—that went out with the Beatles!"

"I don't fancy him!" Lily said. "And besides, the way he looks is the best part of him, trust me."

"Oh, it's obvious he's a complete bore. I don't know how you stand it."

"It's not exactly that." Lily pushed open her front door and motioned for Kimble to go in ahead of her. "It's just that he insults me all the time—tells me how rude Americans are."

"He'll be death to your social life," Kimble said. "I would avoid him like the plague if I were you."

"Who are we avoiding like the plague?"

Mom appeared in the doorway to the living room, a package of Jammy Dodgers in hand.

"Mom!" Lily said quickly. "This is Kimble. I brought her home to meet you."

"Hey, Kimble," Mom said. "Want a cookie?"

She offered the package of Jammy Dodgers. Kimble took two.

"Just so people won't look at you oddly," Kimble said, "these are called biscuits, not cookies."

"Thanks for the tip," Mom said. "They are good, aren't they? But they're better with milk. Will you join us?"

Without waiting for an answer, Mom led the way into the kitchen. Lily expected Kimble to give a scornful look over her shoulder, but Kimble followed Mom, chatting away about what a nice house they had.

She sure knows how to work parents, Lily thought. *I'm sure she lives in a much nicer place than this. I'm sure everybody does!*

Mom got out milk and more "biscuits" and sat at the kitchen table with them.

"Where's the little itch?" Kimble asked.

Mom's mouth twitched. "I see you've met Tessa. She and Joe are out playing soccer."

"She's a bit of a windup merchant, isn't she?" Kimble said.

"I'm not familiar with that term," Mom said. "Enlighten me."

"It's as if you have a key in your back and she turns it until you're going 'round in circles like a madwoman."

Mom actually grinned. "That pretty much describes her."

Kimble leaned forward as if she were about to divulge a secret. "She was the one who practically forced Lily into that boat yesterday," she said. "If Lily hadn't gone, she would surely have drowned. I hope you're not putting all the blame on Lily."

"I'm taking responsibility!" Lily said. She pushed the Jammy Dodgers toward Kimble.

"I think we're over it," Mom said. "So—how was the boy watching?"

"We didn't see a thing worth looking at," Kimble said. "Boys are not what they talk up in the tabloids. I'm thirteen and I'm supposed to have hormones that make me want to look at lovely boys—but it rather bores me, actually."

"Does it, now?" Mom said. "So what does interest you?"

"Clothes," Kimble said. "Cosmetics—I'm mad for them. I love to transform myself in front of the mirror, see how many people I can be. And Lily—

she fascinates me. I've never known an American girl before. She's quite different than I expected."

"How so?" Mom asked. She propped her feet up on the extra chair and munched easily on a Jammy.

"She's not wild. I always thought Americans had a wild streak."

"That's probably because of the way she's been brought up," Mom said.

"And how's that?" Kimble asked.

"She has rules."

"Such as?"

"We meet her friends before she spends a lot of time with them."

"Got it."

"She's not to ride in cars—or boats—unless she has our permission."

"Right."

"She can have boys as friends, but no dating yet."

"Oh, heavens no."

"And she's to do her best and treat us with respect."

Kimble seemed to be waiting. "That's it, then?"

"That's it."

"I wish you would talk to my mum! She has so many rules, I can never remember them all. It's the Magna Carta she has going." She nodded at Mom as if she were giving her approval. "You're good parents. I think I might like to hang 'round here, if you don't mind."

"I wish you would," Mom said. "Come as often as you like, whenever you and Lil aren't running around Oxford—"

"Following the rules," Kimble said.

"Following the rules," Mom said. "Would you like to stay for supper?"

"I would be charmed," Kimble said.

Lily didn't say anything. She just stared in amazement.

Well, right-o! she thought. *Right-o!*

Chapter 9

The next day, Saturday, Mom and Dad announced that on Sunday, the Robbins family would begin its new routine. It was time to get some structure back into their lives.

"Does structure mean we're gonna start school?" Joe asked.

Ever since their dip in the river, Lily noticed, Joe had been less sullen. He must have figured nothing could be worse than being covered in slimy water filled with goose poop. It was either that or the fact that he was picking up English football at a fast pace and had made a friend named Nathan who had skinny legs and said everything was "brilliant."

"Yes, school," Mom said, "and chores and—"

There was a unanimous groan that drowned out the rest.

Sunday morning the family went across the street to St. Margaret's for the ten o'clock service. Lily felt that tug pulling her into the sanctuary again, and on the way out after the service, she thought it might be neat to join the Church of England. She loved the majestic organ music, the green robe the minister put on when he was preparing the Communion, and the candles flickering everywhere. She especially liked the prayers they read together from what appeared to be an ancient book, called the *Book of Common Prayer*. It was like reading poetry out loud — poetry written for God.

"My only problem with it is that they don't have Sunday school," Mom said.

"That's because the kids here get religious education at school," Dad said. "I'll have to see what I can do about that."

On Monday the real routine began, and it was almost the same every day after that. To say that it was different from what they did back in New Jersey was the understatement of the whole century, Lily decided.

To start with, the kids joined Mom and Dad for a sit-down breakfast — something they never did unless they went out to the diner on a Saturday morning — and prayed for a good day. Tessa always started to wiggle before they even said amen.

Then Mom gathered the three kids in the dining room and gave them their school assignments for the day. Lily's were for the whole week, which she actually liked. She'd always dug projects. Then they worked all morning, Joe commandeering the living room, Mom sitting with Tessa in the dining room, and Lily setting up shop in the sunny kitchen. As the days went by, she watched the leaves on the oak tree turn to gold and the vines on the side of the garage become a deep shade of red. It was lonely, though, without Girlz to pass notes to and Chelsea and Ashley to avoid in the halls. She never thought she would miss *them* — but school this way was minus a huge chunk.

That was why Lily looked forward to the afternoons. Mom always made a big deal out of lunch. Sometimes she fixed the kids grilled cheese and soup, and at other times she took them to the Eagle and the Child, the pub where C. S. Lewis and J. R. R. Tolkien, the guy who wrote a book called *The Lord of the Rings,* had liked to hang out. Dad seemed to think that was a big deal. The place allowed children in the dining area before certain times of the day, and it really did have the best fish and chips Lily had tasted yet. She was fast becoming an expert. When Joe found out that bangers and mash were sausage and mashed potatoes, he was all over it. His sulking days seemed to be over.

After lunch they had a required one-hour reading time, which was never long enough as far as Lily was concerned, especially after she started reading

The Lord of the Rings. She had to admit that this English guy could really write. Tessa, on the other hand, "whinged" sourly through it, as Kimble would say, until Mom had to threaten her with no soccer if she didn't hush up the complaining and get her face in a book.

Tessa didn't let the clock go one second past the end of reading hour before she was in Lily's face, ready for "their" time. Mom had suggested that to take the place of Tessa hanging out with Lily and Kimble. It was only forty-five minutes but Lily found herself gritting her teeth through the entire thing.

If they watched a movie on TV, Tessa talked through it, asking more questions than they did on *Jeopardy.* If they went down the street to get a snack from the guy from India who pulled his van up to the curb almost every day, Tessa complained that the kabobs were greasy or begged the man, whose name was Ali, to throw in extra chips, which embarrassed Lily beyond blotchy skin. And each day when Kimble showed up on their doorstep after her school was out, Tessa went into her "no fair" routine until Mom whisked her off to soccer.

Kimble usually came straight from school, still wearing her uniform — a gray pleated skirt, white blouse, and navy blue blazer. She complained almost daily that it was "dreadfully ugly and stodgy." It was all Lily could do not to tell her that at least she belonged somewhere and should stop being such a complaining "whinge."

I've had an earful of her moaning on, she thought. And then she realized how English she was starting to sound, almost in spite of herself.

Some days she and Kimble stayed at Lily's, either up in Lily's room or downstairs with Mom, who Kimble seemed to like almost as much as she liked Lily. Other days they did their tour of Oxford, hitting Boots at least once a week, stocking up on McVities from Sainsbury's, or sprawling on the grass at one of the university parks. Wherever they were, Kimble talked about boys and cosmetics and how she wished they were in London. Lily started to think Kimble was playing a tape — the same one every day.

One afternoon they passed a particularly inviting park and Lily asked to stop there.

Kimble sniffed. "It's rather a shirty place," she said.

"This is gorgey," Lily said. She gazed out over the grass that extended all the way to the River Cherwell, the other river in Oxford.

This time Kimble gave a grunt. "I won't be able to show you any blokes here. L.M.H. is a girls' college." She pointed to a honey-colored building that seemed small compared with the other schools.

"L.M.H.?" Lily said.

"Lady Margaret Hall," Kimble said in a high-pitched voice. "The students here couldn't give a rip about boys."

"Why not?"

"They're all wrapped 'round their causes," Kimble said. "People call them 'lively minded women.' I call them perfect prats."

"I don't know," Lily said. She watched a pair of women in their early twenties hurry through the keyhole-shaped opening in the wall that surrounded the college and felt a heavy longing to be them. "I think it would be neat to have a cause."

"I already have one." Kimble lowered herself to the grass, crossed her long legs in front of her, and leaned back on her elbows. "I'm going to leave this Herbert of a town and live in the city I was meant to be in."

"London," Lily said.

"Don't waste your time in this dull-as-dishwater place, Lily," Kimble said. She flicked at a blade of grass as if she were disposing of Oxford entirely. "The world is in London—and so are the boys." She wiggled her eyebrows.

Lily cocked her head at Kimble. "What are you going to *do* with a boy if you actually find the perfect one?" she asked.

Kimble gave her a long look. "I still have so much to teach you," she said.

Lily squirmed. She wasn't sure she really wanted to learn whatever it was Kimble had in mind.

They had to hurry home on Tuesdays and Thursdays if they were out, because those were the days that Ingram came by, without fail, to continue Lily's Oxford history lessons. He was still something of a "whelk," as Kimble called him. "It's a horrible, slimy, shellfish thing," she told Lily. The good thing was that Mom said Lily could do a project based on what she was learning from him and that could be her social studies lessons. That gave Lily enough reason to bite her tongue and follow Ingram around.

Besides, Ingram was on a mission to take her to every old church in the city. And once Lily was inside one, it wouldn't have mattered if he'd called her a rude, uncivilized barbarian. The rest of the world dissolved around her. It was the one time she felt something besides out of place and annoyed.

It was mid-October before Ingram felt she was "ready" to see Christ Church—the oldest one. That day Lily and Ingram started out in the usual way, with Ingram striding along as if he were headed into battle, and Lily practically trotting alongside him while he filled her in on background.

"Its proper name is the Cathedral Church of Christ in Oxford," he told her. "It's actually the chapel for Christ Church College; the members call it 'the House.'" He glanced at Lily. "You won't want to call it that."

"Yeah, since I'm not a member, I know," Lily said. She fought back the urge to call him a whelk to his face and nodded for him to go on.

"Yes, well, right. The idea of the cathedral—not the building itself—goes back more than a thousand years to the days of the Saxons, which I haven't instructed you on yet."

"I've heard of them," Lily said tightly.

"But what you'll want to know—being a girl—is that there was a rather minor monarch who ruled the district of Oxford, under the kingdom of Mercia, and he had a daughter—a princess, naturally."

"Naturally," Lily said.

"She was known as Fritheswith, which means 'the bond of peace.' Not to rave on too long about this—"

"No, no," Lily said. They stopped at the corner of St. Aldates and the High Street, and she nodded vigorously at him. "I want you to rave. Her name meant 'the bond of peace'?"

"Yes, well, right."

"That is so cool. No, it's beyond cool—it's sacred or something. Okay—go on."

Ingram started to walk again. "She vowed her entire life to God, so her father built her a small church—you'll see the spot. It's all meadows and streams and wooded hills, the sort of thing girls like."

"And that's where we're going?" Lily asked.

"We're going to that site. As I *told* you, the building is no longer there. It's a different building now."

"Right, right—so what else?"

"She founded a convent. They were Catholics then."

"Of course. It was long before the Church of England," Lily said, half to let Ingram know she wasn't an idiot and half to get it all straight in her head. "And?"

"The convent didn't last long. The church burned down in 1002 after some Danes used it to escape the massacre ordered by Ethelred the Unready."

Lily let out a snorty laugh. "Ethelred the Unready? Where did they get those names?" She shook her head. "So—back to Princess Fritheswith."

"The Catholics made her one of the patron saints of Oxford."

"I never understood that whole saint thing," Lily said. "I thought we were supposed to pray right to God—through Jesus, of course."

Ingram slowed down a little and looked at her. His blinking slowed too. "Do you actually pray?" he asked.

"Well, yeah. Don't you?"

Ingram shrugged. "I never saw much use in it, actually."

"Do you go to church?" Lily asked.

"On holidays—and when my grandmother comes to visit."

"Do you believe in God?"

"I suppose." He looked around them at the oranges and golds that emblazoned the trees they were passing. "Something has to be responsible for all this. We might as well call it God."

Lily wasn't quite sure what to say. Ingram talked about God the same way he talked about everything else, as if it were a matter of dates and facts and things to check off on a test. And yet she didn't want to correct him the way she was sure he would correct her if the situation were reversed. She felt bad not defending God—the God she talked to every night—but Ingram was like one of Oxford's stone walls. She *couldn't* be sure that if she told him he was all wrong about God, he wouldn't tell her she was a dolt—in his cool English way. She decided to drop it but it nagged at her the rest of the way.

Once they reached the Cathedral Church of Christ in Oxford, however, all thoughts of Ingram slid away, and once again the rest of the world evaporated with them. All Lily could see and think and breathe was the church before her.

Like the rest of Oxford's buildings, it was made from old stone that shone like honey in the afternoon sun. There were towers of every kind — a square one with square turrets, a domed one with miniature steeples, and a tall pointy spire that rose above the rest.

"The main spire is the oldest in all of England," Ingram said. "Now, you *may* have noticed" — though he sounded as if he rather doubted it — "that every period of English medieval Gothic is represented in the architecture."

"That's why every tower is different," Lily said. And then she hurried away from Ingram even as he was explaining something about the east end being nineteenth-century rebuilding.

Lily pushed open the big doors and slowly entered the cathedral. It was perfectly quiet, and as the door closed behind her, even the college bustle disappeared into a velvety silence. Lily caught her breath as she gazed before her.

Ingram had said it was a small church, as cathedrals went, but the ceiling that vaulted above her in a magical weave of ever smaller and smaller arches made her feel tiny and meek — as if she were standing before God himself. In fact, the whole church seemed filled with a magnificent presence — not the side of God whom Lily wrote to in her journal and who she knew was always inside her, but the side of God she hadn't thought much about. This was the God who ruled over everything.

This is a monument to his bigness, Lily thought. *It's scary.*

With Ingram somewhere vaguely behind her, Lily crept up the aisle, almost afraid to lift her head but needing to take it all in — the great stone columns that dwarfed the seats below ... the marble floor with its green and white pattern ... and ahead of her the altar, drenched in the streaming light from its two stained-glass windows. Lily looked up at the colored glass fashioned into a roselike round window far above it, and she felt a chill. It wasn't a fearful, goosebump feeling; it was more like a thrill — a thrill more exciting even than the thought of going home.

Lily reached out and grasped the first thing her hand came to — a carved wooden railing in front of a long pew. She let it hold her up as she whispered, "Hello, God."

All the way home, while Ingram went on about how the New Bodleian across Broad Street didn't measure up to previous architecture or something, Lily rolled over and over in her mind how she'd felt in the cathedral.

It was even more than what I feel like when I'm in St. Margaret's, she thought. *It makes me want to be like Thomas Cranmer or Princess Fritheswith. It makes me want to have a reason.*

Suddenly her eyes began to tear up, unexpectedly, like a flash flood.

It was bad enough just missing my Girlz and my school and everything I know, she thought. *Now I feel like a nothing.* She had to swallow hard to keep from sobbing out loud and risking Ingram hearing her. *Everybody's right,* she thought. *I really don't know who I am!*

She stopped dead in the middle of the sidewalk, as if right in front of her had dropped something that she couldn't get around. It was the worse feeling yet. She was homesick for herself, and she didn't know where to find her. She was lost.

"Why have you stopped, then?" Ingram asked. He sounded to Lily as if he were very far away.

"I don't know," she lied. "I've just stopped."

"That seems a senseless thing to do."

Lily shook herself back to him. The tears stung her eyes as she glared at him. If he took one more verbal step into her private thoughts, she knew she would slug him.

"Well, that's me, all right," she said between her teeth. "The terribly sense-less American."

"Now, see here," Ingram said, blinking furiously. "I didn't say that."

"Yes, you did. You just said it — just like you *always* do!"

"I never said *you* were senseless. I merely said —"

"It doesn't matter what you say." Lily could feel her eyes flashing, burning away the tears. "Every time you open your mouth, you insult me. You are nothing but a perfect whelk!"

77

The words were out before she could stop them—like angry little Tessa's escaping her control. And the moment they hit Ingram's ears, he stopped blinking. He stopped moving. He stopped doing everything. Across his face went a wave of hurt that washed away all his arrogance. Lily felt as if she'd just stabbed both of them.

"I didn't mean—" she started to say.

But the wave disappeared from Ingram's face and he straightened himself up a stiff inch taller.

"Yes, you did mean it," he said, icicles dripping from his words. "Because you are as rude as my father says you Americans are. You have no sense of propriety, no appreciation for culture and history—"

"Oh, do shut *up!*" Lily cried.

And then she turned on her heel and ran the rest of the way down Woodstock Road to number 5. The presence of God she'd felt so strongly just a few moments before seemed very far away. Only the loneliness for the former Lily Robbins was there, choking her with its fear. All she wanted to do was get up to her room, bury her face in her pillow, and disappear.

But the minute she opened the front door, she heard the clatter of silverware coming from the living room, and Tessa's voice saying, "Why do you wear that scarf on your head? Is that part of being a sister?"

Sister? Lily thought. *Did she mean Sister Benedict? Here?*

Abandoning her hide-in-my-room plan, she went straight to the living room. Not only was Sister Benedict sitting with the rest of the Robbins family, eating store-bought spice cakes, but Mr. Griswold, the minister, was there too. *This must be Dad seeing what he can do about the kids' religious education,* Lily thought.

"I suppose it is part of history, my dear," Sister Benedict was saying to Tessa as Lily came through the doorway. Tessa looked baffled.

"Lilliputian!" Dad said. He waved a teapot in Lily's direction. "You're just in time for tea!"

Lily gulped down the tears she'd planned to soak her pillow with and sat on the lumpy couch next to Joe, who looked as if he too had been coerced into joining the group. Sister Benedict was on the other side of Lily, topping off her cup of tea with cream and dropping several lumps of sugar into it as well.

Dad was holding forth about something, and Sister Benedict silently passed the cream pitcher to Lily as if she weren't listening to him at all. So far Lily hadn't been too crazy about tea, but she dumped half the pitcher into the cup Mom pushed toward her and popped in some sugar. Sister Benedict watched, face twinkling, as Lily tasted it and drained the cup. She felt a little better.

Tessa lunged for the sugar bowl and began a process of loading her tea with lumps of sugar, tasting it, making a face, and adding more sugar. At one point Mom quietly slid the cup away from her before it could overflow onto the floor.

It didn't take long for Lily to figure out why Joe was again looking sullenly bored out of his soccer socks. Mr. Griswold and Mom and Dad were talking about the condition of the Church of England and comparing it with how things were with the church in the United States. In minutes both Lily's and Joe's eyelids were at half-mast and Tessa was practically standing on her head. Then Sister Benedict put her hand on Lily's arm and whispered, "I think we must have our own class, you and I."

Lily jolted out of her boredom. "You do?" she said.

"Perhaps you could come to the church sometimes and we could talk about things."

"What kinds of things?" Lily asked. They were whispering around the adults the way Lily and Reni did in geography class.

"Your pilgrimage," Sister Benedict said.

Lily stared. Mudda had called Lily's year a pilgrimage. Were she and Sister Benedict secretly emailing?

"You are on a very important journey, you know," Sister Benedict said. "It would be an honor to be your guide."

That makes three of you! Lily thought.

The soft gleam in Sister Benedict's faded eyes, however, told Lily that this woman wasn't going to teach her British slang and makeup tricks or try to instruct her in the history of English kings between insults. This tugged at Lily like the tugging she felt in the church.

But other thoughts crammed into her head too.

What if she does turn out to be like Kimble—always wanting to talk about things I don't really care about? What if she starts to think I'm an idiot, like Ingram does, and I end up popping my cork at her? Or what if she's just daft, like she seems when she just appears out of nowhere and says strange things to me that hardly make sense?

"Now that sounds like a marvelous idea!"

Both Lily and Sister Benedict whipped their heads around to look at Dad. He had obviously overheard—the same man who could go for weeks without knowing what was going on at his own dinner table. Lily wanted to scream. Was he going to throw her into yet another situation without even asking her?

"Are you offering to continue Lily's Christian education?" Dad asked, eyes shining behind his glasses.

"It would be a privilege," the old nun said. She had her hand firmly cupped behind her ear, as if she really wanted to get this straight. "But only if the student is willing."

"Of course she's willing!" Dad said. "Lily is our avid learner."

But Sister Benedict was looking closely at Lily, as if Dad hadn't spoken at all. Naturally, before Lily could say, "Can I think about it?" Tessa piped up with, "What about me? I wanna come."

Mom shook her head at Tessa. "You and I will be holding court here, hon. We're going to have to start with Adam and Eve."

Tessa went on to wail about it not being fair, while Joe cackled into his hand—until Mr. Griswold said Joe should come and join his boys' group on Friday afternoons and Dad heartily agreed. Lily could almost see the smoke coming out of Joe's ears.

She looked again at Sister Benedict, but she had her eyes closed and her mouth was moving silently as her thumbs twitched in her lap.

Tessa poked Lily and whispered hoarsely, "What's she doing?"

"I don't know," Lily whispered back. She just hoped it wasn't something weird that she was going to make Lily do when they "had their own class."

Not that it matters, Lily thought, *since it looks like I don't have any choice.*

She couldn't help glaring at the back of Dad's head.

Sister Benedict and Mr. Griswold left soon after that, Dad pumping both their hands and thanking them as if they'd just offered to pay for Lily's and Joe's college educations. By the time the door closed behind them, Lily's plan to escape to her room went back into effect. She had to get away, she thought, or she was going to lose control and explode at Mom and Dad. But she only got as far as the kitchen stairs before Mom read her body language.

"Whoa, girl," she said. "Before you go stomping off in a huff, let's hear what's on your mind."

Lily stopped but she didn't turn around. "I don't want to talk about it," she said.

"That's usually the time when you *need* to talk about it," Dad said.

Lily did turn, just in time to see Mom look at Tessa and Joe, who were settling themselves in at the bottom of the steps and licking their chops in anticipation.

"Out of here, you two," Mom said. "Get washed up for supper."

"I'm clean," Tessa said.

"I'm practically disinfected," Joe said.

"I'm not," Lily said. She talked through the gritted teeth that were holding back tears of anger, an overwhelming sense of being lost, and much more that she couldn't put a name to. "I think I'll go up and take a bath. I don't really want any supper anyway."

"Stay right where you are," Mom said. "And let's talk about this tone of voice you have going on."

"What tone of voice?" Lily asked.

"The one that says you are going to do exactly as you please," Mom said.

"There's no way I'm going to do that," Lily said. "Dad's making all these 'arrangements' for me—then I have to have Tessa under my nose practically every minute, and when I do get some time to myself, I'm hanging out with people who aren't even my friends. I don't have any friends, because you guys decided I needed to be in some foreign country, where I feel like a big old honkin' sore thumb—"

"That's enough, Lil," Mom said. She darted her eyes toward Dad, whose face, Lily saw, looked as if he'd just been slapped.

But it was too late to pull it all back and too hard to stop the rest of it from pouring out. All Lily could think of to do was tear up the stairs and do what she'd wanted to do all along. She turned toward the steps to flee. Tessa's leg came out right at Lily's shin level, and in one flailing ungraceful move Lily was sprawled facedown on the steps, barred from a concussion only by Joe's left forearm, which she caught and carried with her in the fall.

Around her voices swirled.

"Get off me!"

"Tessa—what in the world!"

"She was dissin' me!"

"Lily—are you all right?"

Lily plucked that question from Dad out of the confusion and turned on it.

"No, I'm not all right!" she cried. "And I won't ever be all right as long as I'm in this … this … Herbert of a place!"

There was a long, stricken silence.

"What's a Herbert?" she heard Joe mutter.

"Go on up to your room, Lily," Dad said. His voice was low and flat.

That's where I wanted to go in the first place, Lily thought miserably as she gathered herself off the steps and stumbled up them. *If you had just let me go when I wanted to, this wouldn't have happened.*

But she didn't dare say it. The hurt in Dad's eyes had been replaced with a sternness the Robbins children didn't see there often. Lily didn't know which made her feel worse.

And she definitely did feel worse—worse than the day she'd said good-bye to the Girlz. There was something more going on inside her now, something beyond missing them, something that far surpassed the longing for home.

Lily sank on her bed and hated its lumpiness. She wanted to talk about this—sort it out somehow. She couldn't go to Mudda on the computer—it was downstairs, and judging from the look on Dad's face, she was doomed to stay right here in her room until she started getting gray hair.

She dug under the mattress for her journal. It wasn't in the spot where she knew she'd left it. Frantically she yanked up the whole mattress with both hands, dumping her homemade T-shirt pillows on the floor. The journal was shoved into the frame of springs that substituted for the box springs they had at home. Lily's face began to burn.

If Tessa has been into my private writings..., she began to rant to herself.

But she stopped. There was already too much in her head and in her chest—so much that she couldn't even cry.

And when she opened her journal, she couldn't write either. Not to God, the way she always did. He seemed too big now, after what she'd seen and felt in the cathedral. He was majestic and powerful and she was sure he was disappointed in her.

She closed the journal and pressed it against her chest as she stared miserably outside. A light in a window of St. Margaret's Church winked back at her, and for a "daft" moment Lily thought it might be Sister Benedict herself.

Perhaps you could come to the church sometimes and we could talk of things, the sister had said.

"Perhaps I could," Lily whispered. "Even a daft old lady is better than nothing."

And nothing was just what she felt.

Chapter 10

No one came to Lily's room that night to, as Kimble would have put it, "give her a good rollicking." Tessa came to bed right after supper, mumbled an apology Lily was sure Mom was standing outside the door listening to, and told her there was a sandwich in the fridge for her if she wanted it. Lily didn't. She fell asleep thinking about Sister Benedict, hoping with her eyes squeezed shut that the old nun wouldn't be another disappointment.

As soon as breakfast was over the next morning and Tessa had gone upstairs — under protest — to brush her teeth, Lily approached Mom at the kitchen sink, ready to deliver the speech she'd lain awake putting together. She barely got past, "Mom, I've been thinking about what Sister Benedict said last night," when Mom turned to her without a mouth twitch in sight.

"Go see her, Lily," she said. "You need to do something before you drive us all into an asylum."

"I'm sorry," Lily started to say.

Mom folded her arms across her chest. "Saying you're sorry like it's something to check off a list of must-dos after you've hurt your sister's feelings — and your father's doesn't quite cut it. Especially if nothing changes."

Lily felt a blotchy fire rising on her face.

"I know I'm supposed to excuse most of it as hormones," Mom went on. "But I've never bought that. I know you're doing your growing-up thing, but if you're this miserable and nothing any of us does seems to be right, it starts to affect the whole family and it needs to be dealt with." Suddenly Mom's eyes drooped in a way Lily had never seen them do before. "I thought I could be the one to help you, but maybe the time has come for you to have a mentor or something. By all means, go to Sister Benedict."

Lily was sure she was supposed to try to make Mom feel better — and part of her did want to fly into her mother's arms and tell her she was the *only* one who could help. But the rest of her held back because she knew it wasn't true. She wasn't sure anybody could.

"And if that doesn't work," Mom said, "we'll both just go crazy together. I don't think it'll be a long trip for either of us." Finally her mouth was doing its almost-smile thing, but it didn't make Lily feel any better. She just said, "Thanks, Mom," and headed across the street for St. Margaret's.

Lily wasn't even sure Sister Benedict was available at this hour, and she was inside the church before she thought maybe she should have called first — or at least found out where to find the old nun.

Lily was about to turn, go back home, and start over with a phone call when the church suddenly sprang to life with the sound of voices, saying something in unison. Up in the "choir section" in the front — which, Lily had figured out during services, wasn't really for the choir at all — a group of people had gathered. Some women were in plain clothes; some men wore the white collars she'd gotten used to seeing on the ministers around Oxford. They were all reciting what Lily recognized as a psalm. It echoed through the church, the voices like those of angels whispering to God. Although she hadn't made a sound, Lily put her hand over her mouth and slipped silently into a chair.

When the psalm was over, prayers were said. Then the people quietly nodded to each other and left the church, mouselike, through every door and
archway. Soon the place was once again dark and quiet—except for Sister
Benedict, who hobbled happily toward Lily with her cobweb smile working
double-time. Sister Benedict held out her hand to squeeze Lily's.

"Come with me," she said in her crackly voice. "We'll go someplace more
private."

Lily followed the sister down a side aisle, through an arched doorway,
and then through a maze of arched hallways, until they reached a small door
that opened into a room so tiny, it made Lily and Tessa's bedroom look like a
basketball court. It contained only a neatly made bed, two straight chairs, and
a small table with a row of several candles on it. Yet the room didn't seem like
a cell. There was something warm about it.

"Is this where you live?" Lily asked.

The sister didn't answer. She seemed intent on lighting the candles, and
she wasn't cupping her hand around her ear.

"Is this where you live?" Lily asked again in a louder voice.

Sister Benedict turned from the candles and with her face a wreath of smiling wrinkles said, "Welcome to my home. Sit down if you like."

Lily sank onto one of the wooden chairs, expecting it to be hard, but somehow it molded to her and she rested against the back. Still, she crossed and
recrossed her legs several times and looked at the plain walls and the carved
stone Celtic cross that hung above the bed.

Sister Benedict just sat quietly on the other chair and watched until Lily burst,
"Can you help me, Sister? I'm miserable and I'm messing everything up."

Sister Benedict closed her eyes. "At last," she said, "we are coming to the
next right question. Tell me about your misery."

Lily only hesitated for about half a second before telling Sister Benedict
all about how much she missed her friends, how she wasn't finding a group
of friends here, how Kimble was a friend and yet she wasn't, how ugly things
had gotten with Ingram, how much Tessa was driving her mad, and, worst
of all, how evil she'd been to her parents because she felt they were being so
unfair to her.

"I think I've forgotten how to be who I am," Lily said. "The only time I'm
not wishing I were back in Burlington—that's my town in America—is when

I'm in an old church. When I come out, all I can think of is that I wish I had a *reason*—not just to be here but to be anywhere." She shrugged. "Maybe I'm just getting weird."

"A beard?" Sister Benedict said. She looked curiously at Lily's chin.

"No. *Weird!*" Lily said.

"Oh—well now, that's much better. Weird we can do something about. A beard *would* be a bit of a problem, wouldn't it?"

Lily admitted it would, but she crossed her legs a few more times.

"Lily, love," Sister Benedict said, "you are not weird—or daft, as we would say here, or mad or 'gone 'round the bend.'" Lily stared. Sister Benedict was as good a glossary as Kimble and probably safer. "It is simply that you are on a pilgrimage. Most women are a bit older when they begin, but it is quite obvious that the Father has great plans for you. He wants you to begin early."

Once again the word *pilgrimage* stunned Lily. She resisted the urge to say, *Have you been talking to my grandmother?*

"In my experience with these things," the old woman said, "all pilgrimages begin with a state of deep disturbance."

"That's me—I'm definitely disturbed," Lily said.

"And I believe it began long before you came to England. Something was missing in your life but you didn't know it."

"No! My life was perfect before I came here! This isn't a bad place," she added, "but it isn't *my* place. I think that's why I'm confused."

"It's still the same face—"

"*Place!*"

"—but it is taking on a new shape. And perhaps you had to be away from your friends to allow it to happen."

"What could possibly have been missing? I had everything."

Sister Benedict's face seemed to go smooth and her eyes took on a fine shine. "Did you hear God every day, every hour, Lily?"

"Not every hour—but a lot. Whenever I had a problem and I prayed really hard, I could hear him and I knew what to do. I don't anymore."

"God wants your full attention. Could you give that to him when you were gadding about, organizing your friends and whatnot?"

Lily squirmed. The wooden seat was no longer comfortable. "Does that mean I'm not supposed to go out and have fun with my friends? I mean, we weren't just messing around. We did a lot of *good* things. We prayed for Tessa when she was paralyzed, and helped her with her physical therapy. We got justice for Reni when she was discriminated against—stuff like that."

"That was what you were supposed to do *then*," Sister Benedict said. "It's different now."

"So what *am* I supposed to do now?" Lily asked. "That's what I don't know—and it scares me."

Sister Benedict broke into a smile. "Good!" she said.

"I'm supposed to be scared?"

"No. It's good that you are now asking the right question: What am I supposed to do now, God?"

"I guess I'm supposed to be all happy about this opportunity to be in a foreign country and see all this stuff most kids don't get to see till they're old or something."

Sister Benedict put her finger to her lips and Lily let her words fade.

"That is what your mind tells you. Quiet your mind and let God tell you."

"I don't know how to do that," Lily said. "I'm used to figuring things out."

"Ah," the sister said. "No, that won't work, not in this case. The thing to do is to remain lost and let God find you."

"What?" Lily said.

But Sister Benedict was nodding with her eyes closed, as if she had just cleared everything right up for Lily.

"Shall we pray?" Sister Benedict asked.

"Sure," Lily said. Everything in her was sinking. That was it? That was the "help" Sister Benedict was giving her?

"Father," Sister Benedict whispered, "we beseech you to pour your Holy Spirit on Lily as she begins her pilgrimage, lost and confused and ready to know your will."

Lily squeezed her eyes shut. *Yikes!* she thought. *She's already praying!*

"Let the Spirit empower her," she went on, "and our Lord Jesus Christ guide her. You have begun a good work in her. Please bring her to your holy place. Amen."

Lily opened her eyes to see Sister Benedict watching her. "Would you like to put out the candles?" she asked.

"Okay," Lily said.

The old nun handed her a candle snuffer on a long handle. As Lily placed it over the first flame, Sister Benedict put her gnarled hand over Lily's and whispered, "Jesus, please be the light that guides my way."

She repeated that with each candle. At the last one Lily found herself saying it too.

"Amen, amen, amen," the sister whispered. "Yes and yes and yes."

She didn't say another word until Lily reached the door. And then she only said, "Will I see you again soon?"

"When shall I come?" Lily asked.

"Whenever God sends you," the sister said.

As Lily found her way out of the maze of arches and back to Woodstock Road, her mind was spinning.

Why did I tell her I'd be back? she thought. *She only confuses me.* Yet Lily knew something had settled in her too. *Maybe it was the candle thing. Because I sure don't know anything I didn't know before. Stay lost? I can definitely do that.*

She spent the day as much by herself as she could, except for the time she had to be with Tessa. That part was strained. The two people she really wanted to communicate with were Mudda and Reni.

After she was finished doing the dishes—all the while wishing that Shirty Sheggs had invested in a dishwasher—she went into the dining room to get online. Mom was there, staring at the computer screen and frowning. Lily hoped that it wasn't about her for once.

"Will you let me know when you're done?" Lily asked.

"I'm finished," Mom said. "No email from Art—again. It's been four days. You haven't heard from him, have you?"

Lily shook her head. She hadn't received an email from her brother since the second week they'd arrived. *No wonder I'm lost,* she thought. *He at least made sense sometimes.*

"I called Jane Dooley," Mom said, more to herself than to Lily. "She said he wasn't feeling well for a couple of days and maybe that was why he hadn't written." Mom's mouth twitched only slightly. "If he wasn't feeling well, he'd be on the phone whining to me."

"Yeah, he's a big baby when he's sick," Lily said.

Mom left and Lily sat and typed an email to Reni.

> If I can't be home, I wish you were here. You would un-
> derstand about how I feel when I go into a church, and how
> I just feel lost all the time. I talked to that nun I was telling you
> about. She's pretty cool, though weird. But I can't call her on the
> phone, and she doesn't come over and hang out in my room. I
> want you!

She wrote to Mudda about her talk with Sister Benedict too.

> I don't understand what she means about staying lost and let-
> ting God find me. Won't that just make me and everybody else
> more miserable? I'm sick of that. I can't think of the best part of
> today.

She was just signing off when Tessa yelled from the kitchen, "Phone, Lily! It's Kimble. She says she has something to tell you."

"Tessa — would you zip it?" Joe yelled from the living room. "I can't hear the TV!"

"What's going on?" Dad yelled from atop the library ladder in the same room.

"Why is everyone yelling?" Mom yelled from upstairs.

Lily took the phone from Tessa and sat on the floor in the kitchen with her hand over the ear that wasn't squeezed against the receiver. Another thing Shirty Sheggs should have bought was a cordless phone.

"It sounds as if you're having a ruddy debate over there," Kimble said.

"What's up?" Lily asked.

"I told you not to forget that I am brilliant, didn't I?"

"Uh-huh."

"I am about to prove it to you. I have found two little chums for that blithering sister of yours to hang 'round with, so you don't have to look after her every day of your life."

"You did?" Lily said.

"Of course I did. I looked 'round among the first-formers — they're about eleven years old — and found two that I think can hold their own. Neither of them play footie, so she can't do them any bodily harm on the playing field, and they can both talk your face off, as it were, so she won't be able to dominate the entire conversation, as she is wont to do."

Lily had to laugh. Kimble was talking like Dad. She was hanging around the Robbinses' dinner table way too much.

"So," Kimble went on, "when shall we put these three little urchins together? Tomorrow?"

"You'll have to bring them over here."

"Oh yes, the inspection by Mummy and Daddy. I'll make sure there's no fooling 'round and that neither one of them is showing her tattoo."

"They have tattoos?"

"Just joking. You really need to get out more, Lily. You can't become a bore." Lily could picture her smiling slyly. "But that is the whole point of this, now, isn't it?"

Lily felt a pang of misgiving as she hung up the phone. This sounded sneaky. But on the other hand, this could mean not having to spend so much time with Tessa. It would be one less reason to be cranky, which was getting her into trouble. Feeling a glimmer of hope, Lily did some mental preparation and then approached Mom and Dad, who were up in their bedroom, seemingly in a deep discussion. They interrupted their conversation long enough to listen to her. She hoped she sounded as if she wanted to help Tessa and make things better for the family.

I guess I do, she thought. *But mostly I'm doing this for me.*

Mom and Dad agreed to meet "the two little urchins" — and then looked as if they wished Lily would leave so they could go back to what they were discussing. She just hoped it wasn't her. She kissed them both good night and went to bed still feeling lost.

Sister Benedict should watch what she prays for, she thought.

Then she looked out the window, across the street at St. Margaret's. The light was still burning in the window.

It's always burning, Lily thought.

She suddenly had the urge to light a candle—only *that* would probably cause another family "row," as Kimble would say. Tessa would wake up and want to do it too.

Instead Lily rolled onto her back, closed her eyes, and imagined the little flames flickering in Sister Benedict's tiny room. They weren't Otto and China but they were somehow comforting.

"Just let it shine in me, please, great God," Lily prayed as she drifted off to sleep. "I haven't shined in a long time."

Chapter 11

Kimble showed up at the front door at two o'clock the next afternoon. The two "little urchins" standing with her, who turned out to be identical twins, looked more like little angels, with their rosy cheeks and the big-toothed smiles all eleven-year-olds seemed to have. They even had lovely big bows in their hair.

Oh, brother, Lily thought. *Tessa is going to eat them for lunch.*

She looked doubtfully at Kimble as she let them all in.

"Just remember that I am brilliant," Kimble whispered to her.

Mom and Tessa joined them in the living room, where the two little girls sat side by side on the couch with their hands folded in their laps. Tessa stood behind a chair and looked as if she couldn't wait to tear into them.

This isn't going to be lunch for Tessa, Lily thought. *This is just an appetizer!*

"This is Molly and Maggie," Kimble said, pointing but not differentiating between the two. They were so identical, they looked to Lily like clones of each other.

"Would you girls like some Jammy Dodgers?" Mom asked.

"Oh yes, please," said one twin.

"If it isn't too much trouble," said the other.

Tessa's eyes rolled. Mom's mouth twitched.

"I'll be right back," Mom said.

The minute she was gone, both girls glared at Kimble.

"Look here," said Molly or Maggie. "How long do we have to keep this up?"

"This hair bow is completely naff," said the other. "I feel like a perfect dolt."

Lily looked at Tessa. Her "gob" was slowly spreading into a smile.

"I'm not so sure about this," Lily whispered to Kimble.

"You've got to trust me," Kimble whispered back. To the twins she said, "You only have to win over her mum. Once you're off alone together, you can be your little urchin selves."

One of them stuck out her tongue at Kimble.

"Watch it, Molly," Kimble said. "Or I'll duff you up."

How can she even tell them apart? Lily wondered. They both had the same silky blonde bobs, same enormous blue eyes. They really did look innocent — until they opened their mouths.

"Does 'duffing up' mean what I think it means?" Tessa asked.

"What do you think it means?" Maggie asked. At least Lily guessed it was Maggie. She was the one who hadn't stuck out her tongue. Her specialty seemed to be twisting her mouth into a knot. It was just about as attractive as the protruding tongue.

"I think it means she's going to kick you around the block," Tessa said.

Molly nodded. "Only she just *thinks* she can do it."

"Right," Maggie said. "And frogs are going to jump out of my nose."

Tessa let her grin go all the way, and she plopped down on the floor in front of the couch. First-form chattering began.

"You see," Kimble said, nudging Lily with her elbow. "I'm brilliant. You're practically a free woman already."

"But they're just faking it for Mom," Lily said. "If she knew what they were really like, she probably wouldn't let Tessa hang out with them."

"It's not as if they're *yardies* or something," Kimble said. "How much trouble can an eleven-year-old get into?"

94

Lily looked at Tessa, who was quizzing the twins about the pranks they had managed to pull in school. She wasn't sure what a yardie was, but if it was something that meant trouble, Tessa could be one.

"Okay, Jammy Dodgers for all," Mom said from the doorway.

There was much yes-pleasing and no-thank-youing and elaborate compliments about the way Mom had displayed the Jammy Dodgers on the plate. Lily only ate one—all the sugar in the conversation was making her nauseous. Even Tessa was picking up on the game, saying at one point, "Mom, can I hand you a cookie—or sorry, biscuit. I'm gonna have to brush up on my *real* English."

Of course, Tessa could only keep that up for so long. She finally turned to Mom and asked, "So—can I play with these guys or not?"

"That would be so lovely," Molly said. "We could go to the shops and play in the park."

"Perhaps Tessa could come 'round for tea," Maggie said.

"Well, I'll tell you what," Mom said. "Why don't we have you girls play with Tessa here for a few afternoons, just until we all get to know each other? Then we'll see about going out."

Lily saw the big toothy smiles harden. Molly's eyes shifted to Kimble. Lily could tell she was dying to stick out her tongue.

"That would be lovely," Maggie said. "Do you have a room where we might play, Tessa?"

"I've got a great room!" Tessa said. "I share it with Lily—" She looked at Lily. "Hey, you remember what you always say about needin' space? I need some right now."

Visions of her room being demolished swept through Lily's mind, but Kimble gave her a nudge.

"Go for it," Lily said. "Just—remember the rules."

"Oh, we will," Maggie said.

You don't even know what they are! Lily wanted to say to her. But the trio had already disappeared into the hall, and their footsteps could be heard tromping on the stairs.

"Aren't they sweet little ladies, Mrs. Robbins?" Kimble said.

"I don't know—are they?" Mom said. "What was that all about?"

Kimble looked innocently at Mom, blue eyes wide.

Mom shook her ponytail. "Well, if they can influence Tessa to have manners for even ten seconds, they're worth giving a chance," she said. "But I'm keeping my eye on them."

"You just let me know if there's any trouble," Kimble said.

"Why?" Mom asked. "So you can duff them up?"

When she was gone, Kimble looked at Lily, her eyes still wide. "She doesn't miss anything, does she, your mum?"

"No," Lily said. "She doesn't." Although Mom was obviously already wise to what was going on, Lily still felt guilty—and more than a little annoyed at Kimble.

"Shall we go shopping, then?" Kimble asked. "There's a gorgey new display of London fashions—"

"Wait a minute," Lily said. She glanced at her watch. "Why are you out of school?"

"I wasn't feeling well, so I told them I needed to go home." Kimble smiled her sly smile. "But funny thing—on the way I suddenly felt cured. It must have been a miracle."

Lily felt more confused than ever. She asked Mom if she could go with Kimble and then followed her out the door.

I don't think this is the kind of lost Sister Benedict was talking about, Lily thought. *God—I hope you find me soon.*

For the next few weeks, as October faded its brilliant colors into November browns, things seemed to settle back down at the Robbinses' house. There were no more arguments with Mom and Dad.

It helped that Tessa had friends of her own now. The twins got out of school earlier than Kimble, so they usually appeared at the front door with their plastic smiles a little after two in the afternoon.

"They must really like Tessa," Lily said to her mother one day.

Mom shifted her eyebrows. "Either that or they hate to go home. They don't even stop to check in with their 'mums.'"

"Maybe their mums don't give them Jammy Dodgers," Lily said.

There were drawbacks. Since the trio had become as inseparable as the Three Stooges, a number of Lily's markers had suddenly run out of ink, and

Mom had started buying cheaper biscuits because the Jammy Dodgers were being consumed at an alarming rate. Lily hoped Mom was keeping a *very* close eye on them.

Lily didn't see how Mom could, though, because she always seemed so distracted about Art. He only emailed one-line messages, like, "Fine here. How are you?" That always started Mom tightening up her mouth. Lily kind of knew how she felt, since the Girlz' emails, even Reni's, were getting shorter and shorter too. In fact, Reni's answer to Lily's email about Sister Benedict said,

> I think you're doing one of your things where you go way nuts over something. You remember, like when you wanted to be a doctor and when you gave that party. It always turned out okay, but this is, like, way serious. Why don't you just have some fun? We're having a blast here. Shad's mother took us all on a hayride. Missed you.

It stung so deeply, Lily didn't check her email for two days after that.

It also concerned Mom that Art always seemed to be asleep when she called him at the Dooley's. And when they did get to talk to him, he seemed listless on the phone.

"Is he homesick for us, do you think?" Dad asked one evening when he hung up from trying to get more than two words out of Art.

"He should come over here," Joe said. "This place is cool."

They all stared at him.

"Since when did it become cool?" Mom asked.

"It was always cool," Joe said. "I just didn't know it."

"I think it's cool too," Tessa said. She looked at Lily. "Lily's the only one who doesn't."

"I don't know," Mom said, as if none of the kids had even spoken. "Maybe I should fly back to the States and check on Art in person."

"I think we should give it some more time," Dad said. "This is a huge change for him. I don't think he realized what an adjustment it would be to live without all of us."

Mom just tucked her lips in and nodded. Lily was pretty sure there would be more discussion between the two of them later.

At least Mom's constant thinking about Art meant she wasn't fighting with Lily. But Lily herself was far from okay. She wanted to do what Sister Benedict kept telling her to do in their "classes" together several mornings a week—quiet her mind and let God tell her what he wanted her to do now. But that was harder than it sounded. Kimble was at the front door every day as soon as Lily's free time started, eager to do the same thing they'd been doing for two months.

I need to go back to Christ's Church, Lily thought. *I think I could really hear God in there.*

Once or twice she considered calling Ingram, but the thought of him insulting her made her want to chop her dialing finger off.

One day when Kimble was getting all settled in on Lily's bed with the latest tabloid, Lily said, "Why don't we go over to Christ Church Cathedral today? I'll buy us some McVities on the way back."

Kimble pulled her head up from the fuzzy photo of Prince William and gazed at Lily as if she'd just asked if they could throw themselves into the Thames.

"You want to go to *church?*" she said.

"I went in once and I liked it in there," Lily said. "I want to go back. What's so wrong with that?"

Kimble went back to Prince William. "No one our age does that here," she said, as if that ended the conversation.

Lily's hair suddenly bothered her and she shoved it impatiently behind her ears. "So?" she said. "Do I have to do everything like they do it here?"

"If you want to have a social life, you do."

"I don't have one anyway," Lily said. "Do you?"

Lily wasn't sure where that had come from. Kimble looked up abruptly from the tabloid and pushed it aside.

"What do you mean by *that?*" she asked.

Lily let the answer just come out, the way the question had. "You spend every single day with me. You don't hang out with your friends from school. Every time I see you in town, you're by yourself."

Kimble pulled her neck up as straight as a giraffe. "I have sacrificed my social life to help you adjust here without making a complete fool of yourself," she said. "Without me, where would you be?"

Maybe a little closer to where I'm supposed to be. The thought was a surprise, even to Lily. And needless to say, they didn't go to the cathedral. But when Lily was lying in bed that night, she had time to think about it and she knew it was the truth.

I could find that cathedral on my own, she thought. *And if I get lost, well, that's what I'm supposed to do — get lost and let God find me.*

It was a frightening prospect, but there was a tiny piece of it that was delicious. Lily decided to set out the very next day.

The problem was, of course, Kimble. The next morning Lily figured out that she was going to have to be well on her way to the cathedral before Kimble arrived from school. There was no way to call her and let her know she wouldn't be home. She finally decided a note would be less of a hassle anyway.

Lily planned and studied the map all morning. As soon as reading time was over and the twins had arrived, Lily scribbled out a note to Mom, who was checking email for the tenth time that day, and slipped out the front door. Wrapping her scarf more tightly around her neck to ward off the mid-November chill, she drew up her shoulders and whispered to herself, "Down Woodstock to St. Giles, just as if Kimble were with me."

And then there Kimble was, emerging from the chemist's just down the street. She was looking over her shoulder as if she were a fugitive from justice.

What is she doing here so early? Lily wondered. *She must have cut her last class again.* Annoyance crawled up her spine like a case of prickly heat. *I can't be with her today. I have to do my own thing!*

Lily craned her neck. Kimble had stopped to tuck something into her purse. Barely looking to see if there were any cars coming, Lily darted across the street and scurried into the covered walkway at St. Margaret's. She peered around the end of it and looked for Kimble again. She was headed straight for Lily's house, arms swinging, spiked head held high.

She didn't see me, Lily thought, letting out a long breath. But her relief was only temporary. Any second Kimble was going to knock on the door and Mom was going to tell her Lily wasn't there — it was going to get ugly.

I should have just waited for her to get here and told her to her face, Lily thought. But trying to explain this to anyone was just plain impossible. To anyone, that was, except Sister Benedict.

Lily had already seen her once that day, but she bolted for the church door and hurried among the arches to Sister Benedict's room. She was only halfway there when she heard a crackly voice say, "So God's sent you back, Lily, love."

Lily turned to see that she'd just passed Sister Benedict perched on a bench in the dimly lit hallway. Lily sank next to her, breathing hard.

"Do you read my mind, Sister?" Lily asked.

"No," Sister Benedict said. "If I did, I would know who you're running from."

Lily sighed down at her hands, which she'd flopped into her lap. "It doesn't really matter. I don't think I'm getting anywhere on my pilgrimage. I'm trying, but something always seems to go wrong."

"I'm hungry," Sister Benedict said. She got stiffly to her feet and headed toward her room, adding over her wide shoulders, "Join me."

Lily knew by now that Sister Benedict would pick up the conversation again eventually, and there was no point in hurrying her.

Once they were in her room, Sister Benedict went to her table and lifted the napkin off a hunk of crusty bread which rested on a plain blue plate.

"Are you following all the instructions you've been given through God's people?" she asked.

"What instructions?" Lily said.

"You tell me," Sister Benedict said. She tore off a piece of the bread and handed it to Lily. It was warm and smelled good.

"Mudda said I'm supposed to think of the most important question I asked every day," Lily said.

"Are you doing that?"

"Yes—but it's always the same question: 'What am I supposed to be doing here?' Oh, and then the other one: 'Why don't I feel like Lily Robbins anymore?'"

"Ah," the sister said, her mouth half full. "Go on."

Lily took a bite of bread and chewed thoughtfully on its warmth. "I'm to write down the answers in my journal—that was Mudda again. I haven't been doing that, because I'm not getting any answers."

"Indeed. What else?"

"Um. Hmm." Lily swallowed and pinched another piece of the bread off. It melted in her mouth like pastry. "You said I'm supposed to get so lost that only God can show me the way out."

"I think you've done that at least—though you fight it as if you're afraid it will do your head in."

"I was going to go to the cathedral by myself, but then I saw Kimble coming, so I hid here." Lily ducked her head. "I'm almost glad it happened. I'm sure I would have gotten lost—I don't like being lost!"

"There isn't a soul who does, Lily, love," Sister Benedict said. "But only when we are lost can we be found. God is trying to find you. It sounds like he has been trying to instruct you through people who have been there. Listen to what they are saying."

"But it's not working! That's why I keep coming here."

"All the answers aren't here in this room. You must venture out."

Lily put the rest of her bread on her lap. "I told you—I'm messing up my pilgrimage."

Sister Benedict let out her kid-laugh. "No—you're just becoming more and more lost so that you have to actually *begin* it."

"But how?" Lily switched leg crosses for the fifth time during the conversation and knocked the bread to the floor. "I just wish somebody would tell me *how!*"

"What is it that Mudda and I have done, my dear?" the sister asked.

"I just told you—," Lily started to say. And then she stopped.

Sister Benedict cocked her head like a questioning little bird.

"There was that one thing she said to do," Lily said slowly. "She gave me a bag."

"Did she, now?"

Lily told Sister Benedict about the canvas bag in which she had dutifully put Shad's disposable cameras and the journal and the pen Mrs. Reinhold had given her, and which she had then stuck in the closet. She hadn't even seen it since the day she put it away. All Sister Benedict did was crinkle her crepe paper forehead at Lily.

"Okay, okay — so I kind of forgot about that. But I can just see me carrying it around to the shops with Kimble and having her tell me no one our age here carries a bag like that."

"Kimble is not your pilgrim partner," Sister Benedict said. Her eyes twinkled. "Though she does give you some useful information from time to time. Did you know that you are developing a British accent? I think that will serve you well on your journey."

"Then what?"

"Take the bag and explore," Sister Benedict said. "Explore as you have never done before, because you were so busy taking care of your friends. Go everywhere you can. That is your pilgrimage."

"Dad told me to spend time like that before I found friends," Lily said.

Sister Benedict focused on another hunk of bread. "It sounds like you have been ignoring a lot of instructions God has been trying to speak to you through other people."

"But I thought I'd found friends," Lily said. "Now I don't think so — and I'm scared."

"Good," Sister Benedict said. "Now you can truly begin."

Lily left Sister Benedict, St. Margaret's, and the candles that day with a different question in her head. It was no longer "What shall I do?" but "When can I start?" It was actually Mom who gave her the first glimpse of an answer.

That very night, in a rare moment of peace while Tessa was downstairs getting extra language arts help from Dad, Lily was digging into the bottom of her closet for her pilgrimage bag. She hadn't yet located it when Mom came in with a stack of folded laundry.

"You should have a rope tied around you so we can pull you out if you get lost in there," Mom said. "You're a braver woman than I am."

"I'm looking for something," Lily said.

"Can you hear me if I bring up a sore subject?" Mom asked. Lily groaned into the closet. "I'll take that as a yes. We agreed that your little forays with Ingram were going to form the foundation for your social studies project. But since we're not seeing much of Ingram these days, I'm wondering how that's going to work out."

Lily could hear Mom opening a drawer and moaning. *She must be look-ing in Tessa's sock drawer,* Lily thought as her hand landed on the pilgrimage bag. She pulled it and herself out in time to see Mom dumping the contents of Tessa's drawer onto the bed.

"Oh," Mom said, "I always keep a half-eaten candy bar and an open marker with my socks." She held up a ruined sock.

"Ingram and I had a fight," Lily said. "I don't think he wants to show me around anymore."

"Did you and Kimble have one too?" Mom asked. "She didn't look too happy when I gave her your note."

"I don't know," Lily said. She shifted her eyes away from Mom. "Anyway, Sister Benedict wants me to get out more and see other stuff besides just Oxford. I'm supposed to explore." Lily stopped there. She wasn't sure Mom would understand about being lost on her pilgrimage.

Mom looked back over her shoulder from the trash can, where she was tossing two-thirds of Tessa's socks. "What do you want to see?"

"More churches, mostly. I like the churches a lot."

Mom slowly came to sit on the bed across from Lily. "That is the first real spark of interest I have seen you show in this place, Lil," she said. She searched Lily's face for signs that this was for real. "I think it's time we went on some field trips, then. I'm kind of itching to see more of the world myself." She turned ruefully to the fresh stack of laundry beside her. "I think I need a distraction. I'm getting way too wrapped up in this laundry thing. I never did that at home, did I?" Lily felt herself brightening a little as she shook her head. "I think I'm too knotted up about Art. He's just doing the normal separation thing."

"Do you think we could go to London?" Lily asked.

Mom seemed to have to pull herself back to Lily. "London?" she said. "Eventually. Let's start with some day trips first."

That night Lily didn't try writing to Reni at all, which made her sad. But she concentrated almost happily on her email to Mudda.

Maybe my pilgrimage is really starting. Maybe I'm finally going to get unlost.

Chapter 12

The "field trips" started right away, and for the next several weeks the Robbinses took a day off twice a week, sometimes with Dad along. Secretly Lily called them "legs of my pilgrimage journey." She and Sister Benedict came up with the name together, and it made the sister's face crinkle like a delighted piece of tissue paper.

When Lily told Kimble, the spikes in her hair seemed to stand up in annoyed peaks. They'd done that a lot since the day Lily ditched her, although at the time she'd said she wasn't the slightest bit peeved. "I *do* have other friends," she assured Lily.

"So you won't be available to go 'round with me every day," she said when Lily filled her in on the plan. "Just so you can go off on some school trip that is simply going to do your fruit."

"Do my fruit?" Lily said.

"Drive you mad."

That was one expression Sister Benedict had missed.

"It's going to enrich me," Lily told her firmly. That was what Mudda had said in her last email and Lily liked the way it sounded.

But Kimble waved her off with a red-nailed hand. "London is the only place worth going to if you want to get rich. When you're ready to go there, *then* talk to me. And you must let me be the one to take you, of course. I know London like no one else does."

"I'm so sure our parents are going to let us go to London by ourselves," Lily said with a laugh. So far she hadn't met Kimble's mother, but Lily knew Mrs. Kew would have to be the mother from outer space to even hear of such a thing.

Although Dad had bought a jalopy of a car for the family to use in emergencies—and Joe said it would *take* an emergency to get him in the thing—they usually went on their excursions by train. En route to all their destinations, Lily studied the countryside. Both Mudda and Sister Benedict had said not to disregard anything as being unimportant to her journey, and Lily was really trying to follow instructions now.

As she gazed from the train windows, Lily saw mostly brooding moors, flat, peaceful-looking fields, and once in a while a soft, rolling place. She took it in through fog and rain because the bright, crisp late autumn had turned into gray, sloppy winter almost overnight. Mom said she was going to have to get everyone warmer clothes.

The first trip was to Bath, in Somerset County, where some of the Jane Austen novels took place. Counties, Lily was learning, were very important in England. She decided to start referring to the place where she lived in America as "Burlington County."

There they saw the Great Roman Bath—which was so green, Tessa said it looked as if it were *made* of goose poop—and in a tearoom ate clotted cream on scones, which tasted far better than it sounded.

But it was the magnificent abbey in Bath that pulled Lily in and dissolved the outside world for her again. Bigger even than the cathedral in Oxford, it shone like gold when the sun went down and all the lights came on. The stained-glass windows took Lily's breath away. She wished someone had been there to play the organ, which, as Mom put it, had enough pipes to provide plumbing for all of Burlington Township. Even without any organ music, God was once again there in all his magnificence, and Lily once again yearned for her "reason."

This must be what a pilgrimage feels like, she told herself on the train back to Oxford. *I'm going to get quiet in every church I can until I hear God tell me what I am now.*

It sounded like a direction—and it got Lily digging into her canvas bag for the journal and the silver pen Mrs. Reinhold had given her. There were the four disposable cameras, still unused in the bag.

She could almost hear Shad saying, "What did I buy 'em for, Robbins?"

I'm going to start taking pictures—of my pilgrimage, she answered him in her mind.

Before the next field trip day, Mom bought the girls blazers and new wool scarves and funky hats to wear in the chill. As Lily and Tessa were getting ready the morning of the trip, Lily examined her reflection in the mirror and decided she looked astoundingly British. She was surprised to realize that she didn't mind so much.

"I almost wish I wore glasses," she said to Tessa.

"You'd look a perfect dolt in glasses," Tessa said. She went back to trying to coax her short dark hair into a Maggie-Molly bob.

The next thing we know, she'll be trying to go blonde too, Lily thought. She was going to have to keep a sharp eye on the peroxide. Still, she felt a little pang. There was a time when Tessa had only wanted to be like Lily. It had practically "done her fruit"—but now she missed it a little.

For that day's jaunt the family piled onto a bus—Dad told them it was called a "coach" in England—which took them out into Somerset County and, as far as Lily was concerned, back in time.

She used up one camera snapping pictures of packhorse bridges arched over streams and rivers, rolling wooded hills and county lanes that wound from one village of thatched-roof cottages to another, inns with signs proclaiming that cider and native cheese were being served inside, and red sandstone walls that stood out even in the wintry mist.

But Lily stopped snapping the moment the bus came to a muddy halt and she saw the cathedral at Wells. Once again she sensed something pulling her inside. Feeling like an unimportant servant, back bowed, she crept beneath the high-arched doorway and stood on a vast floor with the space of the Almighty rising above her.

"Hello, God," she whispered.

"Mom—Lily's really getting weird," she heard Tessa say.

"Can't we look at something besides churches?" Joe said, as if from very far away.

It seemed to Lily that he wasn't far *enough* away. She drifted away from him and from the voice of her mom telling them it would just be a few more minutes. A few more minutes weren't nearly enough.

Silently Lily slipped away from her family and walked until she could no longer hear anything except her own footsteps on the stone floor. She was at the top of a wide set of timeworn steps before she realized she was in another room completely, a room that was perfectly round, with a circular bench surrounding a ring of columns in the middle. Lily sank onto it and felt the cold of the stone chilling her sitting-bones. But that was nothing compared with the thrill that was going through the rest of her, just the way it had in every church she'd visited since Christ Church in Oxford.

There was something different this time, though. This time questions spilled out on their own, as if her heart had been dropped on the stone floor and broken open.

"God—will you please find me?" Lily whispered. "Will you please find me and point me in the right direction? I don't need to have a big cause like Princess Fritheswith. I don't have to be burned at the stake like Thomas Cranmer. Will you just help me be real?"

She knew then that she was crying, but no one was there to see her. No reason to hide the tears. No reason to pretend. No reason to be afraid. She let the tears run down her face and the words pour out of her mouth.

"I'm not the old Lily anymore. Reni's wrong—I didn't come here and find a new 'thing' like I would have last year. But I'm not a good daughter like I used to be. I can't even find friends like I used to have—probably because I'm not who I used to be." She heard herself sob. "But do I have to be nothing and nobody forever? Can't you please show me who I am now? Even if it's just an ordinary girl who only has one tiny reason to be here, that's what I'll be if it's what you want. But please don't let me be unhappy anymore."

"This is the Chapter Room, where the church leaders met," said a formal-sounding British voice.

And then there was another voice, loud enough for a soccer field.

"Here you are!" it said.

Lily jumped, banging her head on the column behind her. Tessa was suddenly in front of her, panting as if she'd just scored a goal.

"Shhh, Tessa—you're in a church!" Lily hissed to her.

"And you're gonna be in your *room,* like for the rest of your life!" Tessa said. She didn't lower her voice a single decibel as she planted her hands on her hips. "Mom and Dad are lookin' all over for you!"

Then she turned and ran as if she couldn't wait to get back and report that Lily had been *miles* from where she was supposed to be. Lily took off after her, smearing the tears off her face. At the bottom of the steps she ran straight into her dad. Dad steadied her with both hands on her arms. His face had that concerned-relieved look that would soon turn to relieved-angry if she didn't start explaining.

"I'm sorry, Dad," she whispered. It was the first time in a long while that her "sorry" didn't sound forced.

Dad's relief didn't melt into anger, so Lily took a deep breath and a big chance. "I was feeling God and I couldn't move," she said. "Honest. I mean, I know I haven't been very godly since we came to England."

Dad took her by the elbow and steered her toward the massive vestibule, where she could see Mom practically tapping her toe and Joe wearing the "You're busted!" look on his face.

"Did you get lost or what?" Mom asked.

"Kind of," Lily said.

Dad didn't say a word. Lily pulled her heart away from him and covered it up with resentment.

"Now can we go someplace besides a church?" Tessa asked. "I want some of that cheese."

Lily looked back at the cathedral several times as they headed for the coach, and she stared at it from the window until its spires disappeared. A few more minutes in there and she *knew* God would have told her who she was and where she was supposed to go. But now she knew he was going to.

After that Lily couldn't wait for each new field trip. It was hard that her family didn't know what was really happening to her and that her only hangout friend, Kimble, wouldn't have understood anything beyond the fact that she liked churches. Kimble just went back and forth between pouting that Lily was gone so much and insisting that everything but London was a waste of time.

"You want churches?" she said. "That's a bit off as far as I'm concerned, but they have churches in London—bigger and better than anywhere else. If I were you, I'd be giving my parents an earful until they took me there on the next train."

Although Lily didn't expect *that* reaction from her parents, she did actually ask Mom again. That night while they were doing the dishes, she casually asked if London was on the field trip schedule.

"Don't ruin the surprise, Lil," Mom said.

"Then we *are* going?"

"Surprise. That's S – U – R —" Mom's mouth twitched. "They tell us the best time to go is during the holidays. That's all I'm going to tell you. Breathe a word of it to Joe and Tessa and I'll —"

"Don't worry," Lily said. "I don't want Tessa doing in my fruit over it." Although, she reminded herself, Tessa wasn't talking to her much these days. Ever since the night of the tripping incident on the stairs, when Lily had made that comment about her being a pain in the neck, Tessa had acted as if Lily was in desperate need of deodorant.

"Doing in your fruit," Mom was saying. "Why did I ever want you to go whole hog over England?"

Lily did tell Sister Benedict about London, because she couldn't hold it in and because telling the Girlz stuff like that via email wasn't fun anymore. Zooey had completely stopped writing back. Suzy gave her something that read like a book report about once a week. And Reni just didn't seem to understand anything. Not hearing from her at all was better than reading emails that told Lily she needed to lighten up.

"Your friends don't understand," Sister Benedict told her, "because they are not where you are. They will catch up someday, but you are already quite far along on your path. The Father is pushing you for some reason." She cocked her head of thinning hair, and the light from the candle flames danced in her old eyes. "Perhaps he wants to use you in a large way that you must prepare for now. Ah, but London. How glorious, my girl! Yes and yes and yes."

"Is it?" Lily asked. "Everyone tells me it's where I should be."

"I've only been there once, before I took my vows," the sister said.

"That must have been a *long* time ago," Lily said. "Not that you're that old, of course."

"Lily, love, I am ancient. But I do remember St. Paul's Cathedral."

Lily caught her breath. "Did you feel God there?" she asked.

"Keep losing yourself in your pilgrimage, Lily," Sister Benedict said. "God will find you."

That's it, then, Lily wrote in her journal that night. *She knows I'm going to find my answers at St. Paul's. But I have to keep losing myself until I get there. I can do that. I can so do that.*

And so Lily continued to look and ask and photograph and write as the Robbinses continued their field trips.

When they visited the Cotswolds in Oxfordshire, the same county Oxford was in, Lily took pictures of sheep grazing, and old market towns, and limestone buildings that reflected every change in the light. Mom said it was charming. Joe and Tessa liked the fact that there were stocks on the village green, and Lily wondered if any martyrs had been put there. There were only sleepy country churches in those villages, but even they seemed to whisper of a God so big, he could take anyone where she needed to be. Lily wrote all about it in her journal.

Lily felt more and more hopeful as she peeked into the tiny chapels in Devon and Hampshire and Kent and gazed up in awe at the great spires of Canterbury and Coventry and Salisbury. But she also wished Mom and Dad would hurry up and tell them when they were going to London. She still felt as if she were someone other than Lily, and it was taking its toll.

"Do we have to go in, like, every single church when we get there?" Tessa said the day they were on their way to Warrick Castle.

"Yeah, dude," Joe said. "I'm sick of churches."

He would pick right now to start siding with Tessa, Lily thought. *And what happened to 'Tessa wants to do everything I want to do so she can be like me'?*

Right now Tessa was sounding more like — well, like the twins when they weren't in front of Mom.

It's like I'm the adopted one and Tessa and Joe are the real Robbins kids, Lily thought. It made her sad, yet there was nothing she could do about it. She had to keep searching.

One day when the Robbinses weren't going on a field trip, Lily realized it was after three and Kimble hadn't shown up. She stared out the front window into the dripping December rain every little while until it got dark, but there was no sign of her.

It was funny. Lily was pretty tired of the things she and Kimble did together, and she told Kimble less and less of what she was thinking about. But it was the first time she hadn't come over after school since they met, and it made Lily feel uneasy.

I know I ditched her that one day, she thought as she headed for the back stairs. *I wonder if she's just doing it to get even with me.*

If it had been one of the Girlz who had done that, Lily would have torn up the carpet getting to the phone. But with Kimble she couldn't decide whether it really bothered her or not.

"Where was your traveling buddy today?" Mom asked as Lily passed through the kitchen. Mom was finally taking down the brown-checked curtains, yanking them off the rods as if she were mad at somebody. Her voice didn't show it but her hands were definitely taking out some anger. It was probably about Art, Lily knew. He had not been returning Mom's phone calls.

"She's not really my traveling buddy, Mom," Lily said.

"So you two did have a falling-out after all."

"She just didn't come today," Lily said.

"I can't tell if you're bummed out about it or not."

"I don't *know!*" Lily said — and then she immediately bit her tongue. "Sorry," she said quickly. "I'm gonna go upstairs and read."

"The gruesome threesome is up there," Mom said.

"Oh. Then I think I'll go see Sister Benedict."

"Good idea," Mom said. She sounded to Lily as if she were biting *her* tongue too. "Get a jacket."

"I'm just going across the street—"

"Get a jacket, and get an attitude check too, while you're at it. I can take one of my kids ignoring me but not two."

Lily practically chewed her entire tongue off as she took the front stairs two at a time. *I thought we were over the whole arguing thing,* she thought. *How am I supposed to get along with her anymore?*

But the minute Lily opened the bedroom door, that question was blasted into the land of the unimportant. In front of her was the only thing that mattered. There sat Maggie, Molly, and Tessa in the middle of Lily's bed, heads bent over Lily's open journal.

" 'I wish God would hurry up and show me,' " Maggie—or Molly—was reading aloud.

But Lily's voice was louder. She went straight to a scream. "What are you doing?!"

"Oops," said one of the twins, rather cheerfully. "We've been busted."

"Do you think she'll duff us up?" said the other one, just as gaily.

Tessa didn't say anything. As far as Lily was concerned, she didn't have to. She tilted her chin toward Lily with a jerk that said, "I'm sorry I got caught but I'm not sorry I did it." Fury charged through Lily like a herd of horses.

She thrust her arm out in front of her, and all three of them ducked as if she were taking a swing at them. "Give it to me!" Lily heard herself shout at them. "Give it to me this minute!"

"We're not done with it," Maggie said.

"We just have a few more pages," Molly said.

"Now!"

Tessa snatched the journal out of Molly's hand and flung it toward Lily, its pages splaying in midair until Lily caught it and crumpled it against her chest.

"Now is she going to duff us up?" Maggie said.

"Get out," Lily said. Her voice was lower but her heart was pounding faster, and she could feel her nostrils flaring as she breathed harder.

"It was getting dull anyway," Molly said with a shrug.

"There wasn't a word about a boy in there," Maggie said. "Kimble said you were hot for boys."

"Get out," Lily said between her teeth.

"You needn't be so rude about it," Molly said. But she gave Maggie a nod and they both hurried past Lily in the doorway, only to run headlong into Mom. They dodged her and disappeared.

"What's going on?" Mom asked.

Lily didn't answer but kept her eyes riveted on her sister. "I said get out, Tessa."

"This is my room too!"

"Get out. Get out before I—"

"All right, no threats," Mom said.

She put a hand on Lily's shoulder, which Lily shook away.

"Make her get out," Lily said. "She read my journal!"

"I didn't read it—*they* did."

"Who showed it to them?" Lily said, voice rising again. "Who got into my personal space? *You!* And you're as bad as they are—worse. I trusted you!"

Tessa's lip curled. "You did not! All you wanted to do was get rid of me! You treat me like a goosegog."

"Because you *are* one!"

"Enough!"

That voice was Dad's—but Lily was too far into her anger to recognize that he was at the high end of his own temper.

"Just get out, Tessa!" she shouted.

Mom put both hands on Lily's shoulders then and no amount of struggling was going to get them loose. "Go downstairs, Tessa," Mom said.

"How come I'm in trouble when she's the one screaming at *me?*"

"Go!" Mom and Dad said together.

"I'd do it, kid," Joe's voice piped up from behind Dad. He didn't even sound as if he were gloating. And as Tessa stormed past Lily and wriggled out between Dad and the doorjamb, Lily heard Joe add, "They don't get this mad too often. You'd better—"

"Oh, shut your mouth!" Tessa screamed at him.

There was some stomping of feet and some slamming of doors and then the house went silent. Lily felt as if she were deflating as she sank onto her bed, still holding her journal.

"What just went down in here?" Mom asked.

"I walked in and they were reading my private journal out loud," Lily said. Her voice was toneless now. "I even had it way hidden — they had to dig for it to find it. It wasn't like I left it lying around." Tears came on as she talked, and Lily stopped speaking so she could fight them back. Mom and Dad weren't going to understand, so what was the use anyway?

"It sounded like someone was being killed," Mom said.

They were about to be, Lily thought. But she didn't say it. She laid the journal flat on her lap and smoothed her palms over the open pages to ease out the creases that had happened when she'd caught it in midair. That was when she saw them — the words written in her margins in purple and red and orange marker.

> *What a goosegog!*
> *You're shirty.*
> *How wet can you get?*
> *This is rubbish!*

Lily came off the bed as if she'd been shot from a gun. "They wrote in it! Look at this — they wrote all over my sacred writings about my pilgrimage."

Mom looked down at the defiled page. "That isn't Tessa's handwriting. She should print so well."

Lily could feel her eyes blazing. "Why are you defending her, Mom? She let them do it — she's just as bad!"

"Joe," Dad said, "why don't you go down and deal with Tess?"

Mom just stared at Lily, her eyes meeting Lily's blaze for blaze.

"Why am I in trouble?" Lily asked. "I didn't do anything wrong!"

"You're not in trouble," Dad said — though the solemn tone of his voice didn't convince her. He put his hand on Mom's elbow. "Maybe you'd better go with Joe to make sure he survives. I'm afraid he might take the brunt of it."

Mom looked to Lily as if she would much rather stay and give Lily an earful of whatever was brewing in her mind. If the phone hadn't rung downstairs, Lily was sure she would have. But as it jangled a second time, Mom only gave her one last glance that said, "We'll talk later," and left. Lily sat back down on the bed and tore through the pages of her journal. Almost every page had been abused with a marker. She felt as if she were going to throw up.

"Why is Mom mad at *me?*" she asked. "Tessa's the one—"

"I think she understands why Tessa let this happen," Dad said. He perched on the edge of Tessa's bed, facing Lily. His voice still sounded stern but Lily was too angry to let that stop her.

"And that's my fault?" she said. "I did something to Tessa to *make* her do this? I thought we all had to take responsibility for the stuff we did. I thought that was the rule."

"It is the rule," Dad said. "And technically you haven't done anything wrong, and I'm not going to give you any consequences."

"Gee, thanks."

The instant she said it, Lily began to shake her head, hard, until red curls smacked against her face. "I'm sorry—I didn't mean that."

"Then why did you say it?"

Dad's face was pinched, his eyes genuinely confused.

"Why is it that everybody understands Tessa but nobody understands me?" Lily asked.

"I understand that you're homesick. I've tried to help you make friends."

"It isn't about that anymore! You weren't even listening to me in the cathedral that day—at Wells. You don't even know what I said."

"Lilianna."

Lily caught her breath. Dad never, ever called her that. She felt suddenly hopeless. Her shoulders sagged, cupping her body around her journal.

"You can ask me anything you want—you can talk to me about anything," Dad said. "But do not speak to me disrespectfully."

Lily swallowed hard. There were words in her throat struggling to come out, but she knew if she let them, they would only tangle things up more. "I'm sorry," was all she could say.

"Tessa admires you," Dad said. "She looks up to you—and until we came here, you were someone she *could* look up to. You actually seemed to enjoy it."

He stopped, as if he were waiting for her to answer. Lily couldn't.

"We came here," he went on, "and you seemed to suddenly go out of your way to make her feel left out. I know she can be a—what is it, a goose-something? Your mother and I tried to provide you with some private time to develop your own friendships—but it doesn't seem to have been enough. And it isn't just her."

Dad leaned onto his knees to get closer to her but Lily didn't look at him. She stared down at the top of her wrinkled journal, still clutched to her chest.

"You've been short with your mother. You drove poor Ingram away. Mom says even Kimble isn't coming around as much anymore." Out of the corner of her eye, Lily saw him shaking his head. "We can't do any more than we've done to try to help you make this adjustment. What is it that you want—besides to go home?"

Finally his voice had softened back to that of the Dad she could run to and explain things to—back when she was Lily. She lifted her eyes and saw him studying her, begging her to try again to make him understand what she was looking for.

But even as she opened her mouth to pour it out, the door came open. Mom appeared—face white and pulled tight.

"Paul," she said in a voice Lily barely recognized, "it's Jane Dooley on the phone. Art's in the hospital."

Chapter 13

Things became so tangled for a while, Lily could do nothing but hang on to the ends of Mom's sentences, which stuck out of her explanation like loose threads.

"—has diabetes."

"—was almost in a coma."

"—serious."

"—die if he doesn't receive treatment."

Everyone's reactions added to the tangle.

"No!" was Tessa's. "He can't die. He's not gonna die. He's not!"

"I heard they just take shots and they're okay," was Joe's. "That's right, isn't it, Mom? Isn't it?"

But it was Dad's that tied Lily into a knot. With tears he didn't even try to hide, he said, "Dear God in heaven, this can't be. It just can't be."

Lily went to him and he held on to her in a hug, but she wasn't sure who was comforting whom. That scared her.

It also frightened her that although Mom had been to the emergency room with her, with Dad, with Joe, and with Tessa over the past two years, she had never looked as terrified as she did now. But it was Mom who got herself untangled first and went straight to the phone to see if she could get a flight to Philadelphia. Dad wanted to go with her, but they decided he should stay in Oxford with the kids.

"I don't know how long I'll be gone," Mom said. "But if I'm not back by Christmas, we'll celebrate when I get home."

"Like any of us is thinking about Christmas," Lily said to Joe as they got Mom's suitcases out of the hall closet for her.

"She'll be back in time," Joe said. "Art's okay. He's probably fakin' it or somethin'."

Lily wasn't sure, but she didn't think Art could fake a disease that people could die from. Joe, she decided, was the one who was "faking it," as if pretending it would go away would make it do so.

But it was obvious that wasn't going to happen. By the time Dad, Tessa, Joe, and Lily saw Mom off at the train station the next night, with cards and notes and drawings from all three kids tucked into her carry-on, there had been at least a dozen phone calls from doctors about things like Art's out-of-control blood sugar, his staying in the hospital until he was no longer in danger, and the need for Mom to learn all about how he was supposed to take care of himself.

Lily asked Dad about it on the ride home from the station. "How long is Art going to have to give himself shots and all that? How long till he's cured?"

Dad seemed to grow smaller behind the wheel. "There is no cure, Lilli-putian," he said. "All he can do is try to keep himself regulated so the disease won't damage his body."

"What do you mean *damage?*" Tessa asked from the backseat. She sounded as if she were conducting an interrogation. Lily knew Dad would tell her, but his words sounded as if he had to force them out.

"Sometimes diabetics lose their eyesight," he said. "They can have kidney failure or bad blood circulation."

"No!" Tessa said. "None of that stuff's gonna happen to Art!"

"What are you gonna do about it?" Joe said. "Duff somebody up?"

Lily had the feeling Joe wasn't pretending anymore. That obviously wasn't comforting to Tessa, because when they got back to the house, she went straight up to their room and lay on the bed and banged her feet on the wall. The howling started shortly thereafter.

"Aw, man," Joe said. "Why does she have to start that now?"

"Because she doesn't know what else to do, Son," Dad said.

Dad hurried up the stairs and Lily could hear him closing the bedroom door behind him and talking to Tessa over her screams. Joe marched into the living room and turned on the TV. BBC news was on but Joe didn't change the channel. He just stared with glazed eyes.

Lily wandered into the kitchen and ran her fingers over the pots draining on a dishtowel. Mom had even washed them before she left, and she'd put a long list of instructions on the table.

We might as well forget that list, Lily thought, *because nothing's the same without her.*

A familiar lump took shape in Lily's throat, as if she were homesick. She'd have given anything just then to have Mom standing there, arguing with her over something that now seemed ridiculous.

"Bring her home, God," Lily whispered. "And bring Art with her."

Suddenly it was all too much and it threatened to break through the walls of her chest. Lily snatched up a pencil and pad that were next to the phone and wrote a note to Dad.

I'm going over to St. Margaret's to see Sister Benedict. It's okay—Mom lets me go whenever I need to. I need to.

A cold rain was slanting across Woodstock Road as Lily crossed, coat-less, and found an open side door to the church. By the time she got to Sister Benedict's room and knocked on the door, she was soaked and shivering. She knew the sister's room would be warm and cozy.

But it was actually dark when Sister Benedict finally opened the door. Only the candle she held shed any light into the dimly lit hall. It took a moment for Lily to be sure it was really her. Without her usual scarf, her thin hair stuck out in wisps all over her head, and she was wearing a long white nightgown that dragged the floor. But it was her sunken mouth and cheeks that puzzled Lily.

"Yiyee?" the old woman said.

"What?" Lily said.

"Haat — yer haat?"

"What?" Lily said.

Sister Benedict beckoned her in and shuffled by candlelight to a cup on the table. She fished out her teeth and stuck them into her mouth.

"Ah," she said. "Now I can talk." Her lips were back to normal and her cheeks crinkled into their cobweb of a smile. "Without them I can't speak properly. It's bad enough I can't hear!" Sister Benedict held the candle up close to Lily and looked at her closely. "But I can *see* — and I can see you aren't happy. Sit down, Lily, love. Let me get you a blanket."

She motioned for Lily to sit on the bed, which she had never done before, and wrapped a knitted afghan around her shoulders. Lily clung to it but she was still cold.

"Don't you have heat?" Lily asked.

"There's a hot brick in my bed that keeps me warm until I fall asleep," the sister said. "Now then — what's troubling you, my girl?"

Just as she always could with Sister Benedict, Lily let it all come out. But this time the more she talked, the more miserable she felt.

"I'm a selfish brat," she said. "I was so wrapped up in my own pilgrimage, I hardly thought about Art at all. I thought Mom was giving it way too much attention — thinking there was something wrong all the time. But she was right, and I feel so — selfish!"

Sister Benedict shook her head as she joined Lily on the bed, wrapped in a shawl. "There are some things only a mother can know — so they tell me. And you know, a pilgrimage, though it seems to be all about you, is never selfish in the end, because of what you then have to offer. Unless of course you step on other people along the way."

It wasn't a question but Lily looked for the answer. She sagged even further into the bed.

"I think I *have* walked on some people," she said.

But before she could start to list them, there was a tap on the door.

"I must invest in a bathrobe if I'm to have this much company at night," Sister Benedict said cheerfully.

She made her way to the door. When she opened it, Dad was standing there, a dripping umbrella at his side.

"Sorry to bother you, Sister," he said. "I didn't want Lily to get wet on her way home."

"Too late," Lily said.

"Ah, but it's the thought that counts, now, isn't it?" Sister Benedict said.

She packed Lily and Dad off, and Dad put the umbrella up and hugged Lily to him as they crossed the street together.

"Milk and biscuits?" he said when they were inside their door. "I know where the secret stash of Jimmy Dodgers is."

"Jammy," Lily said.

She didn't feel like eating, but she settled in at the table across from Dad and scraped the jelly off a biscuit with her finger.

"How are *you* doing with all this?" Dad asked. "You've been so quiet."

"I figured Tessa was making enough noise for all of us," Lily said. "And besides, I've been enough trouble lately."

Dad didn't deny it. He just chewed on a cookie as if he were waiting for her to go on.

"I think I've stepped on Tessa," Lily said. "I just had someplace I was trying to get to, but I know I was selfish about her getting in my way."

She was probably bewildering her father, but he just nodded. "And I think I stepped on Kimble too. She's not a kindred spirit like Reni and the Girlz, but I've been kind of mean to her lately."

"Uh-huh," Dad said.

"I don't know — maybe Ingram too. He was evil to me — but I didn't have to call him a whelk."

Dad choked on his biscuit. "You called him a whelk?" he said. Lily wasn't sure but she thought his eyes were twinkling behind his glasses.

"He is," Lily said, "but I didn't have to hurt his feelings just because he hurt mine. It's just that I was trying to find—"

"Trying to find what?" Dad asked.

Lily let her uneaten biscuit fall to the plate. "You'll think it's stupid."

"Try me."

"I tried before."

"At Wells," Dad said. He gave a grimace. "I was too relieved that you hadn't been carried off by a kidnapper to hear what you were sáying. Try me again."

Still, Lily hesitated—until Dad reached across the table and put his hand on top of hers. It was warm and sweaty. "Dads make mistakes too," he said. "But they like to be given a second chance."

Lily couldn't hold back after that. "I thought I was looking for myself," she said. "Only it turns out I've been looking for God. I mean—for God to give me the right answer to what I'm supposed to be doing. So I guess I was looking for both of us. See—it sounds crazy when I say it."

"Anybody on a pilgrimage is a little crazy," Dad said. "That's part of it."

Lily stared at him. "You knew I was on a pilgrimage?"

"I thought as much," Dad said. "I'm on one myself. That's a big part of why I'm here at Magdelan." He leaned closer, his hand still on hers. "I felt selfish too, taking all of you away from home, but I've been on several pilgrimages in my life. Your grandmother introduced me to the idea when I was about your age. I know from experience that when you're looking for God, you always find yourself as you are supposed to be right then. And I knew, when I came here to start my own journey, that being more authentic could only make me a better father and a better husband."

Lily couldn't say anything. She could only look at the dad she'd thought didn't understand her and see blue eyes and red hair and a searching face, just like the one she saw in her own mirror.

"Well, I tell you what," Dad said, letting go of her hand. "I think you ought to continue on your pilgrimage, and I think you can make up some things to the people you've stepped on."

"How do I do that?" Lily asked.

"You can invite them to go to London with us."

Lily felt her eyes widening. "We're still going?"

"One of the last things your mother said to me before she left was to be sure to take you kids on the trip as planned. She doesn't want you to miss the holidays completely."

"When are we going?" Lily asked. Then she shook her head. "I shouldn't still want to go. That's selfish, with Art being so sick."

"What good is it going to do Art for us to sit around here staring at each other?" Dad chuckled. "We wouldn't survive it. Besides, all the instructions are on your mother's list. You don't think I'm going to ignore those, do you?"

Lily could feel herself brightening from the inside out. "So—when?" she asked.

"Day after tomorrow. That's when the holiday starts here. All the students will be leaving. We might as well go too."

"And you think I should invite Kimble?"

"And Joe should take that little Nathan fellow. Now, Tessa—"

Lily put her hand up. "No, Dad, no twins. The three of them would break into Buckingham Palace or something."

Dad nodded solemnly. Then his face darkened a little.

"What?" Lily said.

"Well, if there are going to be that many of us, we'll need two rooms, and I'll need another adult—and it will have to be a woman."

"Oh," Lily said. "What about Kimble's mom? She's probably been to London plenty of times."

Dad shook his head. "Kimble's mother is very ill. She seldom leaves their flat. There's a nurse who takes care of her every day until Kimble comes home and takes over."

Lily was shaking her own head. "That can't be right, Dad," she said. "That's just not Kimble!"

"It's a side she doesn't show, and she doesn't want anybody to know about it and feel sorry for her. Your mother and I only know because we're nosy about our kids' friends and their families."

"Then how come Kimble gets to hang out with me, if she has to take care of her mother? Why doesn't she go straight home from school?"

"School doesn't really end until right before supper, if you count sports practices. Kimble gave up field hockey this year so she could spend time with you. She has no time for friends otherwise. At least that's what her mother told us."

Lily's heart sank in her chest. She sat back against the chair.

"Don't start beating yourself to a pulp, Lilliputian," Dad said. "Kimble made sure that you didn't know, that there was no way you *could* know. She

123

wanted you to see her as the person she wanted to be, the person she would be if it weren't for her sick mother."

Lily's mind spun back to all the times she had seen Kimble coming out of the chemist's, and she shook her head again. "I could at least have asked," she said. "I never even bothered to try to find out anything about her. You see— I've been selfish on my pilgrimage."

"Then we'll see that you have a chance to make up for it," Dad said. "Let's both pray about it and see if we can't come up with another chaperone. Yes?"

Lily nodded but she didn't feel very hopeful as she went upstairs and climbed into bed. She did start to pray, but the other bed creaked and Tessa whispered, "Are you awake?"

"Yeah," Lily whispered back. "Are you?"

They both giggled. Dad must have worked a miracle on Tessa. Two hours ago she'd been banging and howling like a baboon.

"Tessa?" Lily said.

"Yeah?"

"I'm sorry I've been leaving you out."

"Okay."

They were quiet.

"Lily?"

"Yeah?"

"I'm sorry I let the twins do that stuff to your journal. I'm saving up to buy you another one."

"You don't have to do that."

"Yeah, I do. Mom said."

Lily stifled a snicker.

"I miss Mom," Tessa said.

"Me too."

"Not like I do. She's my only friend now."

Lily winced at the pang that went through her.

"Did you go see that sister lady tonight?" Tessa asked.

"Yeah."

"I thought so. Can she only have one friend?"

"No," Lily whispered. "I think she could be your friend too."

And then Lily came up on her elbow. "Tess," she said, "you just gave me a great idea."

Dad had some doubts when Lily told him she thought they should ask Sister Benedict to go on the trip with them. What if she couldn't get around? What if being with all those kids was too much for her?

"Couldn't you just ask her?" Lily said.

Dad grinned. "Oh yes, there's always that, isn't there? Let the woman decide for herself. What a concept!"

Lily didn't say "Du-uh." She just waited anxiously for Dad to come back from St. Margaret's. He returned with a yes.

There was only one day to get ready, and Lily spent part of it calling Kimble and persuading her to come over before school. She wanted to ask her in person—and she wanted it to be special. She had hot cocoa and cinnamon toast ready when Kimble got there, and she served it in the dining room with Shirty's china.

"Why have you put on the dog?" Kimble wanted to know as Lily ushered her to her seat. Her eyes were early-morning baggy, and Lily wondered if she had been up with her mother in the night.

"Eat," Lily said, "and I'll tell you. No, I'll ask you."

"Ask me what?" Kimble said. She looked at her toast. "This is real butter, isn't it?"

"Forget that," Lily said. "Do you want to go to London with us?"

Kimble stopped the toast midway to her lips, mouth hanging open.

"Is tomorrow too soon for you to get ready?" Lily asked. "You can tell your mum it'll be well-chaperoned. Sister Benedict from St. Margaret's will be with us, and my Dad, of course."

Kimble didn't move or speak.

"I hope you're not disappointed that we aren't going alone, just the two of us," Lily said. "But you can still show me things as if we were by ourselves."

Kimble set the toast down, and slowly, slowly her face broke into the first real smile Lily had ever seen on it. She looked as young as—well, a thirteen-year-old.

"Now, see here," she said, "you aren't trying to do in my head, are you?"

"No," Lily said. "This is for real. My dad will talk to your mum—he'll get it all arranged." She knew Dad was going to pay Kimble's way because her mother couldn't afford it right now—but he'd said Kimble didn't have to know that.

"This is just—this is just mad!" Kimble said.

And then she threw her arms around Lily's neck. Lily was too stunned to even hug her back before Kimble pulled away.

"Don't tell anyone our age I did that," she said. "We don't paw each other like you Americans."

"Then I guess I have a lot to teach you," Lily said.

Once again Kimble smiled at her.

That afternoon, after Lily was packed, she glanced into Tessa's suitcase, which was bulging on the bed.

"Do you want some help with that?" Lily asked.

Tessa brought her eyebrows down to her nostrils. "What's wrong with it?" she said.

"Nothing," Lily said, "except that you can't get it closed. What have you got in there?"

"Stuff," Tessa said. She let go of the scowl. "Mom usually tells me what to pack. I didn't know what I was supposed to bring, so I just packed everything."

"I could help you pick some stuff," Lily said.

Tessa eyed her suspiciously. "Just so you don't try to be Mom. You're not her, you know."

"Promise," Lily said. She opened the bag and pulled out ten pairs of socks and five pairs of jeans. They were only staying two and a half days.

Tessa sat on the floor and propped her elbows on the bed, chin in hands. "I miss Mom," she said for about the twentieth time that day.

"Yeah."

"But what I said last night—it's not exactly true now."

"What was that?" Lily asked. She extracted Tessa's soccer shoes from underneath three pairs of pajamas.

"You're my friend too—I mean, if you still wanna be. You probably don't—"

"I probably *do,*" Lily said. She made it a point not to look at Tessa, who she figured was probably having a hard enough time getting all this out. "Even if you are a little pain in the neck."

"And even if you are as bossy as Art."

They looked at each other sadly and stayed sad long after they climbed into bed—the same bed. Missing Mom and worrying about Art hung heavily over their heads.

But by morning their excitement had returned, especially when Dad came in with presents—early Christmas presents, he called them, since Christmas was only five days away. There was a small backpack for Tessa and a super-deluxe map of London for Lily.

"I knew you'd be carrying that canvas bag," he said to Lily when he and Joe were leaving to pick up Nathan. He looked a little uncertain. "I didn't know what to get you for your journey."

"You did good, Dad," Lily told him.

The only problem was that the map was too big to fit into her pilgrimage bag. After fifteen minutes of packing, repacking, and folding the map every way it would bend, she turned to Tessa.

"Would you carry it in your backpack?" she asked Tessa.

"I guess," Tessa said, snatching it eagerly out of Lily's hand.

"Just stay close to me all the time," Lily said. "I have a thing about getting lost."

"*You* do?" Tessa said. "I thought you weren't afraid of nothin'."

"Anything."

"Yeah, that's what I thought."

A horn blasted from below. Tessa bounded to the window while Lily struggled to zip up her sister's backpack.

"It's Dad," Tessa said. "He's got Nathan and—hey, why is *he* in the car?"

"Who?" Lily asked. She craned her neck to see over Tessa's head.

"Him," Tessa said. She pointed down at the sidewalk, where Ingram was climbing out of the car—with his suitcase in hand.

Chapter 14

Lily snatched up her suitcase and her pilgrimage bag and hurtled down the steps with them. Her mind was screaming, *What is Dad thinking? What is he thinking?*

By the time she got to the sidewalk, both the van-like cab they were taking to the train station and Kimble, laden like a pack mule with three bags and a purse, had arrived. Kimble's eyes looked accusingly from Ingram to Lily and back again.

Lily gave her the only look she could wear just then, which was completely baffled. She dropped her bag and suitcase next to the cab driver and hurried over to Dad, who appeared to be searching his pockets for something.

"Dad?" she whispered.

"Lilliputian, have you seen the—"

"Why is Ingram here?"

"I thought I put them with my passport—you kids all have your passports with you, yes?"

"Da-ad!"

"Ah—here they are, right where I put them." He held up eight train tickets and for the first time looked at Lily's face. "What's the matter?" he asked. "You've lost your passport? Americans always need their passports when traveling in a foreign country."

"No!" Lily stood on tiptoes to get close to his ear. "Why is Ingram here?"

Dad looked at her in bewilderment. "Didn't you want him to come?"

"No! He's a—well, you know what he is! And Kimble can't stand him!"

Dad took off his glasses and chewed on the earpiece. "I could have sworn you said you wanted to make up for all the tromping on people you'd done."

"I do—but I didn't mean for you to bring him along on this trip!"

Dad put his glasses back on and his eyes firmed up out of their confusion. "There's nothing I can do about it now. I've invited him—he's here, ready to go. What would you have me say to him?"

Go back home! Lily thought. But she knew Dad was right. Now, whether Kimble was going to understand it was anybody's guess. And how Ingram was going to treat her was an even bigger mystery.

A crackly voice broke into her thoughts. She looked up to see Sister Benedict crossing Woodstock Road with a canvas satchel over her shoulder. Her smile was bigger and more childlike than Tessa's.

"Sister!" Dad said as he took off at a Dad-run toward her. "We were going to come pick you up!"

"I'm making a bit of a trial run," Sister Benedict said. "If I can't make it across the road, then I can't make it through London, now can I?"

Out of the corner of her eye, Lily saw Joe and Nathan exchange glances.

"Brilliant," Nathan said.

Ingram went politely to the curb to "help" Sister Benedict step up the four inches to the sidewalk. The sister looked amused and proceeded to introduce herself to him. Lily took that opportunity to hurry over to Kimble, who was still giving her the "What is he doing here?" look.

"It got all messed up," Lily whispered to her. "I told Dad I wanted to make it up to Ingram for being mean to him, and he thought I meant invite him on the trip."

Kimble's eyes narrowed into points. "Is that why you're taking me?" she asked. "To make it up to me for sometimes treating me like I'm some sort of Slack Alice?"

"That's not the *only* reason," Lily said.

"Splendid," Kimble said. "I simply can't wait to hear the rest of them." She hitched one of her bags onto her hip and called out, "Tessa! Come make yourself useful and carry one of these to the cab—there's a pet."

Lily sighed and went over to Sister Benedict, who was watching the driver put the bags into the boot as if she were at the circus.

"Trouble, Lily, love?" she asked.

"So far this leg of my pilgrimage isn't going very well," Lily said.

"Embrace the obstacles," Sister Benedict said. And then she turned to the driver and told him, "Well done, my good man. Well done!"

"Brilliant," Nathan said.

Thinking how gross-me-out-and-make-me-icky it would be to "embrace" Ingram, Lily spent the cab ride to the train station, trying to quiet her mind and find God. She didn't hear him, but looking across at Ingram, she didn't feel like being hateful either. In fact, she felt a little sorry for him. He was actually wearing a necktie. She could tell it was keeping Nathan and Joe entertained.

On the train Kimble sat with Tessa, and Ingram attached himself to Dad like Velcro. Nathan and Joe of course were Siamese twins and quickly found something else to snigger about besides Ingram's wardrobe. Lily settled in next to Sister Benedict, but they didn't talk of spiritual things. Most of the time the old sister had her face pressed to the window and tossed excited comments over her shoulder at Lily. "Do you see these charming villages, Lily, love? Everyone has those things on the tops of their houses—everyone. What are they?"

"You mean the satellite dishes?" Joe called from across the aisle. "*We* don't have one."

"Keep looking out the window," Dad said. "You'll see a show out there that you can't find on the telly."

And then he went back to enchanting Ingram with little-known facts about the life of C. S. Lewis.

Dad was right. The scenery between Oxford and London was a show in itself, with stone walls and hedges lining the train tracks, and several large estates whose mansions hid among the trees. Lily was surprised at how much more interesting it was to her now than it had been four months earlier when they'd ridden the train from the airport to Oxford. Genuine excitement was tickling at her spine.

"I don't hate it here anymore," she said to Sister Benedict.

"Of course not," the sister said. "This is where you are supposed to be."

"I'm going to find my answer in London, aren't I?"

Sister Benedict's face grew quiet. "When you're ready to hear it, Lily, love," she said. "At the moment when you're ready to hear it."

About two hours into the journey, after Tessa had made her fourth trip to the loo and the boys had eaten all the snacks Tessa and Lily had packed the night before, the villages gave way to a grayer, more crowded kind of environment. Houses seemed to be stacked on top of one another, and the few gardens the train sped past looked more than just wintry. It was as if someone had given up on them long ago.

The anticipation in Lily's spine fizzled a little. She leaned forward and tapped Kimble's knee.

"Does all of London look like this?" she asked.

"Oh, heavens no," Kimble said. She straightened herself up importantly and seemed to forget that she was punishing Lily with her silence. "We're not there yet—just you wait."

Lily tried to feel reassured, because, after all, Kimble knew London. But what she was seeing looked frightening, like what Dad called "the less savory side" of Philadelphia, which she'd seen when he had gotten them lost. Mom usually checked to make sure the car doors were locked and the windows were up. At those times she *didn't* make Dad stop to ask for directions. Lily definitely didn't want to end up in "the less savory side" of London either.

As they drew nearer to the train station, Dad got them busy collecting their belongings and listening to instructions. He explained that since it was too early to check into the hotel, they would put their bags in lockers there in the train station and start their tour of London. They'd come back and get them later, after dinner.

"Brilliant," Nathan said.

"Thank you," Dad said.

"Where are we going first?" Tessa asked, slinging her bag up onto her shoulder and smacking Ingram soundly in the stomach with it.

"You okay?" Lily asked him.

It was the first time she'd spoken to him since they started out. Ingram looked away from her, blinking, and said, "I'm perfect."

"In whose dictionary?" Kimble muttered to Lily.

Lily didn't feel like laughing, so she didn't. Kimble stretched up so she could see Dad, who was hauling one of her bags down from the luggage rack.

"Harrod's first, Dr. Robbins," she said.

"What's Harrod's?" Joe asked.

"It's a store," Ingram said. He pronounced it as if *store* were a four-letter word.

"No way!" Joe and Nathan said together.

"I would certainly vote against that," Ingram said.

"You're so weird, dude," Joe said to him, but he high-fived him.

"Let's get off the train before we discuss this," Dad said. He hauled yet another of Kimble's bags from the rack. "Whose is this?"

"That would be mine too," Kimble said.

"You're going to need a porter, hon," Dad said.

"Could I?" Kimble asked. "That would be cracking! *Real* travelers use a porter."

Sister Benedict looked at her lone satchel and grinned at Lily. Lily grinned back. She almost wished she'd asked Dad for a bigger pilgrimage bag so she could have brought only that.

Dad managed to get all eight of them off the train, into the terminal, and freed of their bags before anyone wandered off. Lily, for one, was making sure she could see him at all times. In spite of the delicious anticipation, it was hard not to chew on the fear of getting lost.

Finally they were all sorted out, and Dad circled them up in front of a tobacco shop. It was the only store in Paddington Station that didn't distract anybody in the group from what he was saying.

"First of all," he said, looking at Kimble, "Harrod's isn't on our list."

"What list?" Tessa said.

"If you'll recall, I came to each of you and asked you what one place you absolutely had to see while you were here. I've made a list of those."

"Drat," Kimble said. "Why did I try to impress you and say Buckingham Palace instead of Harrod's?"

"Haven't you already seen Buckingham Palace?" Lily asked her.

"So first we have the Tower of London—Nathan's choice," Dad said before Kimble could answer.

Nathan and Joe high-fived each other. Ingram didn't seem to mind the choice either.

"We're going to a tower?" Tessa said, lip curled. "We've seen about a bajillion towers in Oxford."

"Not like this tower," Ingram said. "This is the most famous fortress in Great Britain, and it was once the famous prison Middle Gate. Countless royals and noblemen were imprisoned there until their heads were lopped off."

"Cool!" Tessa said and she fell into step with Ingram.

They had to take the subway—known as the London Underground, or the Tube—to get to the Tower, which meant getting day passes for everyone. Lily tucked Tessa's into her backpack for her and made sure the map Dad had given her was still in there. It was, along with four McVities wrappers. Mom would never have let Tessa get away with eating that much candy.

She was glad Dad seemed to know how to navigate from the confusing map of the Underground on the wall. They got to the Tower with no trouble.

It was, to Lily, a foreboding place, and Sister Benedict seemed to feel it too. The old woman leaned on Lily's arm, murmuring prayers to herself as they went up the wide walkway over the river and into the imposing stone-block building with its barred windows. Shiny blue-black ravens as big as Otto sat on railings and windowsills, staring with menacing directness out of their beady eyes. And the guards didn't look any less ominous. Lily was afraid to open her mouth, for fear she'd be thrown into one of the tiny cell-rooms to await the lopping off of her head.

I'm glad this isn't part of my pilgrimage, she thought. Then she reminded herself that hers was going to have to wait while she did the unselfish thing and let everybody else enjoy. *I don't know if they're on pilgrimages,* she thought as she watched Kimble hungrily eye a fellow tourist of about fourteen who had a pierced nose, *but I guess everybody's on their own journey at least.*

It was a good thought, she decided. She'd have to share it with Sister Benedict later—by candlelight.

It was hard to tear the boys away from the display of armor and swords, but Dad said there might be time to come back to it later. From there they took a red double-decker bus and rode on the top, where it was obvious no sensible English person was going to sit in the damp December cold. Lily loved letting her hair blow back. Kimble closed her eyes in bliss too, though she didn't have enough hair to even be ruffled by the wind.

Their destination this time was Piccadilly Circus—Tessa's choice. She was disappointed to find out that it wasn't a big tent with clowns and acrobats but a square famous for its array of neon lights. She perked up, though, when they ate lunch in a place that had every kind of pizza imaginable, and then made a stop at a toy store. Sister Benedict could hardly contain herself and played with everything she had time to pick up. Even Kimble and Ingram seemed to be eating it up. Ingram challenged Joe and Nathan to a sword fight with toy swords, and Kimble developed a fascination for a doll that came with cosmetics.

When Lily grew restless, she dug into her pilgrimage bag and pulled out a wad of pound notes she'd saved. There was enough to buy Kimble, Ingram, and Tessa—the people she'd "tromped on"—each a huge lollipop. That was all she could afford, and even that nearly emptied her stash. But it was worth it to see them riding in the Tube, licking away. Ingram licked very politely but she could tell he was into it. Joe and Nathan of course bit off hunks of the ones Dad bought them, in a contest to see who could finish first. People stared. Lily stopped caring.

In the midst of the licking and the stickiness, the group saw Joe's choice, the 320-foot Clock Tower of Big Ben presiding over the Houses of Parliament, and Kimble's choice, the changing of the guard at Buckingham Palace. Joe and Nathan did their best to make the guards laugh in spite of Ingram's assurances that they would never so much as twitch.

Between bus stops they passed Trafalgar Square, with its beautiful fountains and huge Christmas tree, and the Monument, which Ingram told them was built to commemorate the Great Fire of London, which started in 1666 and raged for five days, leaving two-thirds of London devastated.

"Does that mean it was totally wasted?" Joe asked.

Ingram assured him that it did. From what Lily could tell, he liked being Joe and Nathan's tour guide, even if they did still make the occasional remark about his necktie. She was surprised by a pang of envy.

She was also surprised by Sister Benedict's choice—it was not Westminster Abbey or St. Paul's. It was a place called The Old Curiosity Shop, which she told them Charles Dickens had written a novel about. She didn't even want to go inside, she told Dad. She just wanted to drink it in from the outside. So Dad hired two horse-and-buggies and they all piled in. Their cheeks were ruddy from the cold by the time they stopped in front of the old place so Sister Benedict could see it.

"I've read about it over and over," she said in an almost-whisper. Then she clapped her hands and said, "All right!" and that was that.

"I always wondered why you wanted to hang 'round with a religious old guinea fowl," Kimble said to Lily as Dad herded them all into a shop to have their tea and get warm. "But she's really rather quaint. I wonder what she'd look like with some cosmetics."

They had all consumed enough scones with clotted cream to feed a small country when Tessa asked, "What's your choice, Dad?"

"Hyde Park," Dad said, "but I thought we'd save that for tomorrow."

"Then we can go back to the Tower now and check out the armor and stuff!" Joe said. He and Nathan, of course, high-fived.

"But what about Lily's choice?" Tessa asked. "We haven't gone to her place yet."

Joe left his high-fiving hand in midair and frowned. "What do you want to bet it's a church," he said.

"St. Paul's Cathedral," Dad said. "Good guess, Joe."

"That took the brains of a pigeon," Kimble muttered to Lily.

"Do we all have to go there?" Tessa asked. "No offense, Lily, but when you've seen one church, you've seen 'em all."

"And we've definitely seen 'em *all*," Joe said.

"I didn't hear all this complaining when you wanted to see the Tower of London," Dad said.

"Yeah, but that was cool!"

"It's okay, Dad," Lily said. "As long as I get to see it, I don't care if nobody else wants to come along. It isn't everybody's thing."

There was a unanimous stare, as if Lily had just announced that she would be sacrificing her right arm as well. Only Sister Benedict looked unsurprised.

Dad finally broke into an "I get it" smile. But he shook his head. "I can't let you go by yourself."

Sister Benedict raised her gnarled hand. "I can chaperone that bit of a jaunt, Paul," she said. "Isn't that why you've towed me along?"

"Can you girls get there all right?" Dad asked. "You'd have to take the Tube—unless I sent you in a taxi."

"We could take Kimble," Lily said. "She's been to London lots. She knows her way around." Lily turned to Kimble. "That is, if you want to go there—you don't have to."

Kimble gave the three boys a disdainful look and said, "I think church is clearly the best choice."

"Okay, then," Dad said. "I'll take Joe, Nathan, Tessa, and Ingram. We'll meet you at the hotel for dinner at—say, eight o'clock? We fellas will pick up the luggage and get it there, so you don't have to go back to the train station."

Lily felt herself beaming. Without everybody standing around looking at their watches and sighing because she'd been in the cathedral five minutes, she was going to have a real chance to find what she was looking for. Finally the day began to feel like a pilgrimage. She had a feeling that Sister Benedict would take care of Kimble so Lily could have some alone time.

"Dr. Robbins?"

Ingram's voice broke into her thoughts.

"Would you mind terribly if I went with them? I've never actually been in St. Paul's."

"Of course," Dad said. "We want you to have a good time."

Dad, no! Lily wanted to shout at him. *He'll ruin everything!*

But Dad was so busy pounding Ingram on the back that he didn't see Lily's face crumpling the way she knew it was. Lily looked helplessly at Sister Benedict, but she seemed completely unaware that there was a problem. She was smiling and nodding at passersby as if she were the hostess of all London.

"Hey," said a voice in Lily's ear. It was Kimble. "I'll keep the whelk out of your road," she said. "Don't fret about it." Then she turned to their foursome and said, "All right—on to the Tube!"

As they headed for the stairs that led underground, Lily thought of her map, tucked safely into Tessa's backpack. But Dad and his crew were already out of sight around the corner.

We'll be fine with Kimble, Lily thought. And she hurried after the rest of her group.

Once they were on the train, zooming at breakneck speed through the dark tunnel, Lily made a head count, the way Mom would have done. Ingram, she noticed, was sitting on the other side, several rows up.

"Ingram," she said. "We're supposed to stay together."

He looked over his shoulder, his eyes pointed straight at Kimble. "I like the company better up here, thank you."

Kimble drew herself up like a large carnivorous bird. "What do you mean by *that,* Mr. Smeg-head?"

Lily looked at Sister Benedict. As the adult in charge, it was pretty much up to her to nip this in the bud, wasn't it? Mom would have.

But Sister Benedict just looked back at Lily, eyes wide, as if to say, "Go ahead, Lily, love. Break it up."

Lily turned back to Ingram, who was doing the "Who's going to blink first?" thing with Kimble.

"We need some ground rules," Lily said.

"Who is going to make them?" Ingram asked.

"Me," Lily said.

Ingram blinked.

"I've let both of you lead me 'round by the nose for too long. This is not the way we do things."

Ingram blinked about a thousand more times, but he didn't argue.

"We're going to a sacred place," Lily went on. "While we're on the way there and on the way back, there will be no insults or other ugliness. We're each of us on our own journey, and we don't get to tromp on other people on the way." She took a breath. "Like I've done with both of you in the past, and like you've done to me, and like you're now doing to each other."

Kimble folded her arms. "Are you quite through?" she asked.

Lily nodded and felt her chest start to cave in. The words had just flowed out of her. They'd seemed so right. It was going to be hard to take if Kimble decided to give her a good rollicking.

But I just feel it, Lily thought. *I feel like I know what I'm doing.*

"Huh," Kimble said finally. "Well, it sounds reasonable to me." She looked at Ingram, who was tightening his necktie. "How about you, Genius?"

"I am rather a genius, in fact," Ingram said.

"I know. That's why I called you that. But are you smart enough to follow Lily's ground rules?"

"What happens if I don't?" Ingram asked.

"I duff you up," Kimble said.

Ingram nodded. "Yes, well, right. I'm on board, then. Let's carry on."

Then he gathered his skinny self out of the seat, came back to where they were sitting, and sat properly in the seat across the aisle.

Kimble nodded as if the whole thing had been her doing. "Yes, well, right," she said.

"Yes and yes and yes," Sister Benedict whispered.

The train stopped not long after that and most of the people in their car got off. Lily looked at Kimble but she didn't make a move to follow them. Lily settled back and savored the prospect of walking into St. Paul's. She hadn't even researched it to see what it was going to look like. She wanted it to be all about the experience of feeling God.

But even *her* imagination couldn't occupy her forever. The train went on for what seemed like hours, letting off the very last of the camera-carrying tourists and letting on more and more people with lunch boxes and tired faces.

"These people must all live near the cathedral," Lily said in a low voice. "They look like they're coming home from work."

Ingram cleared his throat. "Yes, well, right. I don't mean to call your knowledge of these things into question," he said, blinking at Kimble, "but are you quite certain we haven't missed our stop?"

The train began to squeal again as it slowed down, and Kimble stood up abruptly. "This is it," she said.

"Yes!" Lily whispered to Sister Benedict as they shuffled off with a crowd of men and women who looked much less enthusiastic than she did. She was pretty sure they weren't headed for the cathedral.

Kimble led the way up the stairs to the sidewalk above. Lily closed her eyes right at the top so the first thing she saw when she opened them would be St. Paul's.

"Point me toward it, Kimble," she said.

"Toward what?" Kimble said.

"The church! Turn me toward it so when I open my eyes, I can see it."

"Yes, well, right," Ingram said. "You'll have to have superhuman vision, then. There isn't a cathedral within ten kilometers of here."

Lily's eyes sprang open. Through the cold drizzle all she could see on all sides of her were gray, dripping buildings crammed together like the work-weary people who hurried past them, some of them casting hostile looks in the direction of four tourists standing there in the rain.

Lily looked at Kimble. "Where's St. Paul's?" she asked.

Kimble looked back at her, and her face worked up into a burst of tears. "I don't know!" she cried. "I've never been there before. I've never even been to London before!"

The words hit Lily in the chest, and what they meant squeezed her heart until it hurt. Her worst fear had been realized. They were lost.

Chapter 15

"I had a feeling that you hadn't a clue," Ingram said to Kimble. "But since I was told to button up—"

"Shut it!" Kimble barked back at him, tears streaming down a face that was already wet with rain. "Just shut it, before I—"

"Okay, knock it off, both of you!" Lily said.

They fell silent and looked at her expectantly, but that was as far as she could get. Lily glanced at Sister Benedict, but she had her eyes closed and was muttering softly to herself.

Now's a fine time to pray! Lily wanted to say to her. *We're lost, for Pete's sake.* And then her thoughts stopped, tumbling over each other like clowns in her head. *Of course. What better time to pray?*

Lily put her hand up, even though neither Ingram nor Kimble was saying a word. Kimble was trying to pretend that she wasn't crying, and Ingram was adjusting his now very damp necktie.

"Just give me a minute," Lily said. "I'll think of something."

Edging closer to Sister Benedict and beginning to shiver in the bone-chilling rain, Lily closed her eyes and tried to get quiet. She could feel her heart slowing down and her thoughts beginning to take sensible shape. This was the only thing to do. Sister Benedict had said it again and again—when you're the most lost, that's when God finds you. And how could they possibly be more lost than in this less than savory part of a strange city in a foreign country?

Lily caught at her breath and forced herself to calm down. Nothing had changed except where they were.

So I'm not lost on the inside, she thought. *That has to mean something.*

One thing it meant, she was sure. She wasn't as scared, and that made her feel as if she could do something. Forcing a smile, she looked up at Kimble.

"Well," she said, "you wanted us to go to London by ourselves, didn't you?"

"Not here!" Kimble said. "I fancied us in some fine restaurant."

"There's a fine one," Lily said. She pointed to a dark hole of a place whose only light was a purple neon sign that read, "Embassy Pub."

"They certainly have delusions of grandeur," Ingram said.

"That's a pub," Kimble said.

"It's before closing hours for kids," Lily said. "It's better than standing out here in the rain. They probably have a phone."

"You're mad," Kimble said. "There's likely to be criminals in there — all sorts of evil people."

"No more than there are out here," Ingram said.

Only then did Lily notice that Ingram's face had gone a good deal paler, if that were possible. He pulled up the collar of his jacket and blinked nervously at a passing pair of boys, clad from neck to ankles in black leather, with cigarettes soaking at their lips.

"Yes," Sister Benedict said, "let's get a bite to eat, shall we?"

She nodded for Lily to lead the way, just as if they were about to be shown to a table with a white linen cloth and three forks at each place. Lily splashed across the street with the three of them behind her and ducked into the Embassy's dark door.

For a long moment she couldn't see anything. But she could certainly hear. Music from the eighties was blaring so loudly, it rattled the umbrellas in the stand near Lily's leg. By the time they were all in the doorway, Lily's eyes had

141

grown accustomed to the light. She saw they were standing in a short narrow hall that led to a single room with a bar on one side and a collection of tables crowded together across from it. There was a bedraggled Christmas tree in the window; on it was only a strand of garish lights that looked as if Otto had put them on. Here and there a much-used strand of silver garland had been thrown up wherever it would attach. The place looked more suitable for planning a robbery than celebrating Christmas.

A man behind the bar looked up and growled out of a reddish bloated face. Everyone at the tables turned to stare at Lily and her group, and it crossed her mind that it was just like in one of those old cowboy movies when the good guy walks into the saloon.

Lily had to scream to be heard over the music, but she stepped forward and said in her best British accent, "The *sister* and the rest of us want to order some food." Then she held her breath and waited to see if her emphasis on Sister Benedict's religious status would have the desired effect.

Suddenly the volume dropped dramatically and the red-faced man behind the bar said, "Good evening, Sister. Can I help?"

Behind her, Lily could feel Kimble grabbing Lily's coat and holding on as if she were about to drown. Ingram mumbled, "They must be paying off the health inspector on the side."

But Sister Benedict beamed across the pub at the bartender and said, "As my young friend said, we would like a bite to eat. Have you any supper?"

There was a disgruntled scramble among the customers and a table was quickly emptied. Mr. Red Face started to call out the entrees, but a woman with a stained apron waved him off, took a small chalkboard off the post it was hanging on, and brought it over to their table.

"Bangers and mash tonight," she said, pointing. "And kidney."

"This is nice of you to come to our table," Lily said to her. "Don't we have to order at the bar?"

"No trouble, missy," the woman said. She glanced at Sister Benedict.

"You see," Sister Benedict said to Kimble. "There are some benefits to being a religious old guinea fowl."

Lily thought Kimble's eyes were going to pop out of her head. Lily dug into her pilgrimage bag to check her cash supply. She breathed a sigh of relief. According to the price listed on the chalkboard, they could afford two orders of bangers and mash and split them, and that would leave enough for a phone call.

"Two bangers and mash," she said. She was pretty sure nobody would want the kidney. "And water for all."

"I'll buy us a round of cider," Ingram said.

"How lovely," said Sister Benedict. "It's for all the world like the loaves and fishes."

Kimble nudged Lily's elbow.

"Would you look at that?" she whispered, hot breath in Lily's ear. Lily looked where Kimble was nodding. "Don't let him see you're looking!"

"Who?" Lily hissed back. And then she saw him—a boy of about sixteen with the very large lips Kimble seemed to "fancy," staring at Kimble as if she were a mannequin in a shop window.

"He should take a picture," Lily whispered. "It would last longer."

"I'm going to the loo," Kimble said suddenly. She snatched up her purse. "I hope I remembered to bring my panstick." She stood up and leaned down to Lily. "Do I have a spot on my chin?"

"No!" Lily said. She rolled her eyes as Kimble hurried off to the restroom. They were lost in London, and there was Kimble, freaking out about a pimple because there was a boy in the room. Lily glanced again at Lips. He looked like one of the kids who spent half their lives in detention back at Cedar Hills Middle School.

Lily returned to the situation at hand. By then Dirty Apron Lady was putting their order on the table, and Ingram was already sipping cider from a jelly jar. The other customers had gone back to their own business, but several had put out their cigarettes, and nobody was talking loud or cussing. Thank heaven for Sister Benedict.

Lily looked at her watch.

"It's only seven o'clock," she said. "Dad won't start to get worried about us until he gets back to the hotel. If I can find a phone, I'll call there and leave a message."

"Excellent plan," Sister Benedict said.

"He hasn't a cell phone?" Ingram asked.

"My mom took it with her." For a second Lily considered calling Mom but she quickly dismissed the idea. *Like she's gonna be able to do something from across the ocean,* she thought. She shook off the uneasiness that started to rise in her and said, "Did anybody hear Dad say what hotel we were staying in?"

Sister Benedict shook her head happily and went back to her mash. Ingram's head-shake was a little more grave.

"Didn't you?" he asked.

"No," Lily said. "He marked it for me on the map he gave me." Her heart sank a little further. "But that's in Tessa's backpack."

"Yes, well, right," Ingram said.

He was looking paler by the minute and blinking harder. Lily was surprised that he wasn't more help. *I guess a genius isn't necessarily good in a crisis,* she thought.

It seemed to Lily that Sister Benedict was too busy enjoying herself to be very concerned. And Kimble was in the little girls' room, preoccupied with Lips — who by this time seemed to have disappeared.

She's gonna be way disappointed when she comes out, Lily thought — which was fine. They had to concentrate on getting word to Dad before he called out Scotland Yard. She was pretty sure that was the British FBI or something. She'd heard it on some TV show Joe had started watching since they'd been in England.

"Do you want some of this, then?" Ingram asked.

He was holding out a forkful of sausage. Lily took it without thinking. It burst greasily in her mouth — and actually tasted spicy and good. She was feeling more English — and more sure of herself.

"I'm not really that scared," she said to Sister Benedict, mouth half full.

"Of course you aren't," the sister said. "You are no longer lost."

Lily looked around. "I have no idea where we are!"

"But you are home in here," the sister said, pointing to Lily's forehead. "You are using the things God has taught you."

"I don't get it," Lily said. "I didn't learn about any of this in Wells Cathedral or—"

"God merely showed you his almighty presence in the churches, Lily, love," Sister Benedict said. "But his teaching has been everywhere. How else would you have known that children would be allowed in here at this hour? Or that squabbling people must have ground rules? Or that your gifts as a leader are there when the situation calls for them?" Her eyes twinkled. "Or that using my nun status and pretending to be British would be clever ideas?" Sister Benedict gave the pub a flourish with her hand. "You have arrived at your pilgrimage destination."

"Here?" Lily said. She looked around at the dingy walls, the tacky Christmas decorations, the grease bubbles popping from the sausage. She shook her head at Sister Benedict. "No one makes a pilgrimage to a pub, do they?" she said. "This isn't a sacred place!"

"But this is." Sister Benedict pointed this time in the direction of Lily's heart. "Something different is happening in here, I suspect."

Lily took that in. She definitely wasn't afraid, not even in this sinister place. And she did suddenly have an idea.

"Here's what we can do," she said to Ingram and the sister. "If we could get back to Paddington Station before Dad and the boys and Tessa, we could meet them at the lockers."

"Don't count on her to get us there," Ingram said, jerking his head toward the hallway that led to the loo. "She can't even find her way out of the W.C."

"She *has* been in there for quite some time," Sister Benedict said. "Do you suppose she's all right?"

"She's probably totally redoing her makeup—," Lily started to say, but she was interrupted by a scream that ripped its way out of the bathroom hallway and over the music and the buzz of conversation. Lily stood up and shoved the chair out behind her.

"Kimble!" she cried.

Knocking the chair completely over, Lily hurled her way among the tables and dove into the hallway. There was only the light of a naked bulb hanging from the ceiling, but it was enough for her to see the top half of Kimble's face over the shoulder of a figure who had his back to Lily. He had a screaming Kimble shoved against the wall.

"Get off me! Lily — somebody — help me!"

"Get away from her!" Lily shouted over Kimble's cries.

She flung herself against the male back and dug into his shirt with her fingernails. He whipped halfway around. A pair of big snarling lips spat out a curse as he gave Lily a shove with one hand. Lily reeled and landed on her back on the floor, with her head sticking out of the hallway. Deep, raucous voices rose from the pub patrons.

"What the devil?"

"The girl's hit the deck, she has!"

Lily drowned them out with her own screams. "Help Kimble! He's attacking her — help her!"

Somebody picked Lily up by the armpits and sailed her out of the way. She was still screaming when seconds later two men with bulky shoulders and furious faces dragged Lips from the hallway and threw him like a bucket of water out the front door. It slammed behind them, and Lily didn't bother to wonder what was happening on the other side. She squirmed away from the man who was holding her and ran to Kimble as the biggest man yet carried her to their table.

"Put me down!" Kimble cried.

The man deposited her into her chair and retreated to his own table, where two women almost as big as he was toasted him with their mugs.

"Is she all right, then?" the waitress asked.

The bartender hovered, his ruddy face now the color of a meatball in marinara. "Does she need a doctor?"

"Take her to the hospital!" somebody else called out.

"No!" Kimble said. "I'm perfectly *fine!*"

She had her Kimble-voice back and her eyes were flashing.

"It's okay," Lily said to the crowd. "She's just scared."

"Scared?" Kimble said. "I'm ruddy *mad!*" And then she looked at Lily, her face crumpled, and said, "Why aren't I more like you, Lily? If I were like you, this wouldn't happen to me."

She buried her face in Lily's shoulder and sobbed.

"She's fine," Red Face announced to the rest. "When women start crying, they're fine."

There was general agreement, though most of them continued to watch Lily's group over their mugs and plates of kidney.

Lily spent the next thirty minutes calming Kimble down with sips of cider and assurances that she was just as good as Lily any day of the week. Ingram even pointed out that she'd barely smeared her lippy in the fray. Kimble was just beginning to smile when the waitress came to the table and stood there, wringing her hands in her apron.

"Everything all right?" Sister Benedict asked, patting the woman's arm.

"Can we get a taxi for you?" Dirty Apron Lady asked. "It's time children were out of the pub. That's the law."

Lily looked at her watch and groaned. It was too late to head Dad off at the train station.

"Your plan is dashed, I suppose," Ingram said.

Lily nodded. "I just wish one of us remembered what hotel we were staying in."

Kimble raised her head. "I do. As if I would forget! It's Claridge's. I've always wanted to stay someplace elegant like that. I've read that the doormen wear top hats."

"Why didn't you say something before?" Ingram asked.

"It never came up."

"She was in the loo when we talked about it," Lily said. She looked up at Dirty Apron Lady. She was still watching Lily, as was everyone else in the place. "Does anyone know what train we take to get to Claridge's?" Lily asked.

"Well then, aren't we the classy lot?" one man said.

"Shut it, Fred," said the woman he was with. She stood up. "We can't let the sister and these children take the Tube at night all the way back there. Come on — empty your pockets. We've got to get them a taxi."

There were no arguments. Lily watched in amazement as men and women who looked as if they could spend their evenings waiting in back alleys to attack unsuspecting tourists turned their pockets and purses inside out and presented Lily with a wad of money.

147

"Here, little missy," the woman said to Lily. "You keep close watch on this. Fred, don't sit on your duff—get a taxi!"

Fred was already whistling for one before he got out the door.

"My father will probably be there when we get to the hotel," Lily said to Mrs. Fred. "He can give the cab driver money to bring back here to pay you back."

"As if it would ever get here!" someone shouted.

They all laughed as if they'd been wanting to laugh for hours.

"It's a gift, lovey," Mrs. Fred said to Lily. "Happy Christmas."

There was much clinking of glasses then and cries of "Happy Christmas," which even Ingram joined in with. Lily noticed that at some point he had taken off his necktie.

A moment later Fred burst in the door and announced that their taxi had arrived. Lily thought he must have flung himself across the hood or something.

She climbed up onto her chair and yelled, "Thank you—all of you! Good-bye!"

But the crowd left their tables and followed the little foursome out to the sidewalk. One of the men who had escorted Lips from the pub was opening the back door of their cab for them. The other was peering into the window at the driver. His face darkened through his stubbly beard.

"I don't like the looks of him," he said through his teeth to the bartender. "I think I'll ride along."

"Brilliant," said Mrs. Fred. "Then you can come back and tell us they've been delivered safely."

Broad Shoulders nodded as if he'd just been given an official assignment and slid into the front seat next to Ingram. Broad Shoulders Number Two was waiting for Lily to get in the back with Sister Benedict and Kimble.

But Lily hesitated. Mom and Dad's warnings about getting into vehicles or vessels with strangers echoed in her head.

"Not to worry," Mrs. Fred said from the curb. "Bill will get you there safely—I can vouch for him."

Lily grinned at her and nodded. She really didn't need Mrs. Fred's reassurance. She was feeling very quiet inside.

Although Bill urged the cab driver to "hurry it up" about every other block, it was still nearly nine-thirty before they arrived at Claridge's Hotel. Halfway there Lily realized she should have called and left a message for Dad that they were on their way, but everything had happened so fast. It didn't surprise her that when they said good-bye to Big Bill and raced past the doorman and into the lobby, there were several bobbies—the policemen with the nightsticks swinging from their belts—clustered there. Among them was Dad, whose face was whiter than Ingram's could ever have hoped to be.

"There they are!" Tessa cried.

She hurled herself at Lily, nearly knocking her flat onto the thick carpet that engulfed Lily's feet. It was definitely softer then the floor at the Embassy Pub, and it made Lily want to cry.

"Man, where you been?" Joe asked, though he *didn't* hurl himself at Lily. He instead turned to Dad. "I told you they were just out messing around somewhere."

"Brilliant," Nathan said to him.

"We weren't messing around, Dad," Lily said. "Honest. We got lost."

"I don't care," Dad said, pulling Lily into a hug. "I don't care if you robbed a bank, as long as you're here."

"Someone said we'd robbed a bank?" Sister Benedict said. "No, no, that's not true a-tall!"

There was a lot of sorting out to do, which happened after Lily's drenched group had hot baths and gathered over a pot of hot cocoa in the room Dad was sharing with the boys. There was a seemingly endless supply of Jammy Dodgers. Before they started, Dad announced that Mom had called.

"Art has been stabilized. He and your mother are going to be in Oxford the day after Christmas."

"Boxing Day," Ingram put in.

"How long is Art stayin'?" Joe asked.

"Until we all go home in August," Dad said. "He's even going to Paris with you."

"Paris?" Lily said.

"You kids and Mom are going for a month in April."

149

"You lucky dog," Kimble said. "Paris is my favorite city, next to London, of course. I know Paris like—" She stopped. Ingram, Lily, and Sister Benedict *all* blinked at her. "Well, I know it from books. I've always *wanted* to go there," she said.

Then Ingram, Kimble, Lily, and Sister Benedict told about everything that had happened to them that evening, except Kimble's tangle with Lips. Lily gave them the sign and then filled Dad in on it later in the hall outside the girls' room.

Dad's face went very sober. "We'll have to tell her mother, of course. Not so she'll be punished. We just don't want this kind of thing happening ever again."

"I don't think it will, Dad," Lily said. "Kimble doesn't really want to be like that."

"It can be hard to change."

"Not to worry, lovey," Lily said. "We're going to hang out together a lot from now on, only I'm going be my real self ... my new self ... well, the self I'm starting to find."

"Sounds like a tall order," Dad said. He kissed Lily on the forehead. "Do me a favor, though, would you, Lilliputian? Don't forget to be your kid-self too. I miss that."

That Lily wasn't sure she *could* pull off—not after arriving at the destination of her pilgrimage.

But when she opened the door to her hotel room and was plastered in the face with four pillows and a whole choir of shrieks, she picked up Kid-Lily without *even* stopping to think about it.

It was still dark the next morning when Lily heard a crackly whisper in her ear saying, "Wake up, Lily, love. St. Paul's awaits us."

Lily only let her eyelashes flutter once or twice before she bolted upright in the bed.

"We're going to St. Paul's!" she said.

"Shhh!"

Sister Benedict gently patted Lily's lips with her fingertips, but there was a giggle in her voice. She seemed to have rediscovered the art of girlish giggling the night before as the four of them shared secrets and stories and stashed-away McVities.

"First there is something you should see," Sister Benedict whispered. She nodded toward the window, where she had pulled back one side of the heavy drapes—the ones Kimble had said last night *must* have been made from one of the queen's old gowns.

Lily climbed out of bed and padded across the carpet. Sister Benedict pressed her finger to the window. Lily's eyes followed where she pointed, and she let out a gasp.

There, rising majestically above all the other rooftops that came between it and where Lily stood holding her breath, was the dome that had to be St. Paul's. The golden lights that brought it to life in the dark were still on as morning began to tinge the sky with gray. It shone for Lily like a golden beacon across the city.

"It's beautiful," Lily breathed rather than said. "It's every bit as beautiful as I thought it would be." She shook her head. "Ingram told me that when it was built in the seventeenth century, it was meant to dwarf the rest of London, but the city has grown so much that it doesn't do that anymore. I think he's wrong—for once."

Sister Benedict nodded thoughtfully as she too gazed out the window.

"Is it like you remember from the olden—well, the last time you saw it?" Lily asked.

"Oh yes."

Lily rubbed her still-sleepy eyes as she looked at her. Sister Benedict's face wasn't crinkly and lit up. It looked solemn, in fact.

"Are you disappointed that we didn't get to go inside?" Lily asked.

"No," said the sister. "And we *can* go and have a look if you'd like. Your father gave me the means for us to get ourselves a taxi this morning if we want to go before the others wake up."

Lily was sure she would explode with the joy of *that* suggestion. She felt the urge to hug Dad and tell him what a cracking father he was to think up the plan, but as she gazed back at the cathedral, she suddenly felt as sober as Sister Benedict looked.

"It'll still be here the next time we come to London," Lily said. "It's pretty enough from here."

"You don't want to go inside and hear God tell you exactly what you're doing here?"

Lily looked quickly at Sister Benedict. *Now* her old face was crinkly with laughing-lines.

"Was I lame, thinking that was going to happen in *any* church?" Lily asked.

"Bless the good Lord, no!" Sister Benedict said.

She lowered her voice as she glanced at the two sleeping bodies on the other bed. But from the way Tessa's mouth was hanging open and Kimble was snoring soft snores, Lily was sure they were hours from waking up, no matter how loud she and Sister Benedict talked.

"It did happen, Lily, love," Sister Benedict went on. "Little by little in every church you went into. Not because it was a church—but because that was where you did your listening."

"So it could happen in other places too?" Lily asked.

"It already has."

"In your room at St. Margaret's."

"That's one place." Sister Benedict tapped Lily's forehead with a gentle old finger. "Where else did you quiet yourself and know just what you were supposed to do?"

Lily only had to think for the smallest piece of a second.

"Then the Embassy Pub really was the destination of my pilgrimage," she said.

Sister Benedict nodded as she made her heavy way to the nightstand and picked up a candle and a book of matches that said, "Claridge's." She set both on the windowsill and lit the candle. It lit up the window, casting their reflections in light as golden as the cathedral's.

"That depends on whether you now know some answers," the sister said.

"I didn't hear anything then."

"Sometimes it takes some time to discover them even after they come."

But Lily was already nodding. "I think I know one now."

The sister nodded.

"You said I bring out the best in people. I wasn't trying to do that — it just happened."

"It happened when you were doing what you knew to be right. That's the way the soul works, Lily, love. I have told you before, you are far, far ahead of most young people in their connections with God — and themselves."

Lily frowned. "Dad told me last night not to forget my kid-self."

"He's a wise man, your father."

"So how do I know when to be what?"

"God, of course," Sister Benedict said. "Whenever you don't quite know and you begin to feel — awkward."

"Like a geek," Lily said.

"Get quiet and listen for God. He'll show you somehow, sometime, somewhere."

Lily nodded and looked back at St. Paul's. The golden lights were gone and only the thin sunlight glanced over its now gray walls. She had to admit she was a little disappointed that God hadn't spoken from the heights of one of the churches she'd visited, telling her she was to be a saint like Frithenwith or a martyr like Thomas Cranmer. But this feeling she had now — it felt like happiness. It felt like peace.

"Which is it right now, Lily, love?" Sister Benedict asked. "Kid or pilgrim?"

"Right now," Lily said slowly. "I want to wake those two by putting ice in their beds — that'll teach them to keep me up half the night."

And then she stopped and looked at the candle. Sister Benedict blew out the flame.

"Jesus, please be the light that guides my way," they both said.

"But I think I'll always be a pilgrim," Lily said.

"Yes," Sister Benedict said. "Yes and yes and yes."

As Lily watched the candle smoke rise, the words rose in her mind: *Jesus, please be the light that guides my way.*

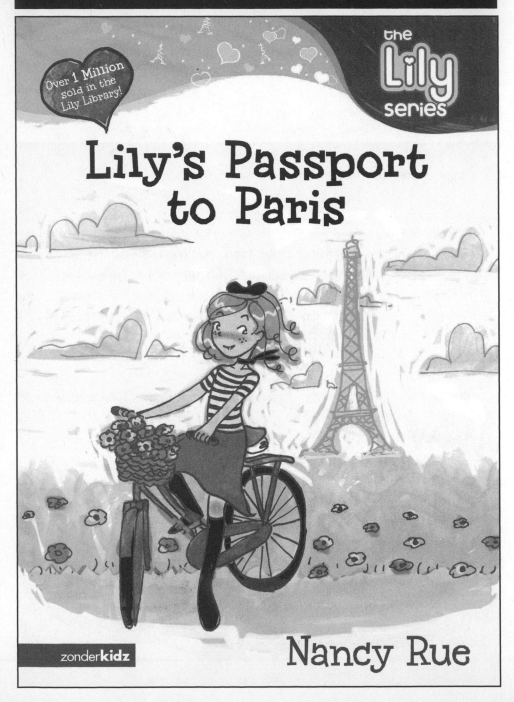

the Lily series

Over 1 Million
sold in the
Lily Library!

Lily's Passport to Paris

zonderkidz

Nancy Rue

Chapter 1

U h, Lil," Lily Robbins' mom said from the back door. "You've picked a strange time to garden, hon." She glanced at her watch. "Our train leaves in an hour and a half."

Lily tried not to give her mom the *I-am-so-not-gardening-right-now-Mother* look and instead held up the plastic Ziploc bag she'd just filled with Oxford soil.

"I'm just getting some dirt to leave in Paris," she said.

One corner of Mom's lips twitched into her almost-smile. "Don't they have enough there?"

Again Lily controlled her face, and she smothered a sigh too, just to be on the safe side of attitude.

"It's a spiritual thing. Mudda told me I should do it."

"I definitely wouldn't question your grandmother—bizarre as the woman can be sometimes." Mom blinked. "Did I say that?"

"Nobody'll ever hear it from me," Lily said. She got to her feet and brushed the dirt from the knees of her jeans—or at least, she tried to. English spring dirt was practically mud, and it stuck to denim like Elmer's Glue.

"I hope you didn't pack all your clean clothes." Mom's mouth was twitching again. "I'm assuming you're all packed."

"I am."

"How many journals did you cram in there?"

Lily couldn't stifle the sigh this time. "Only two—in my suitcase."

"And in your backpack?"

"One. But I need them, Mom!"

"And you're going to need a chiropractor too." But before Mom could say more—and Lily was sure there was more—there was a yell from inside the house that turned Mom immediately on her heel. When Lily's adopted ten-year-old sister, Tessa, let out a bloodcurdling scream like that, she was either winding up to belt Joe or getting ready to hurl some frustrating object against the wall. Lily suspected it was the suitcase Mom had told Tessa to pack.

Betcha she can't get it closed, Lily thought, as Mom disappeared inside the back door. The last time Lily had seen it, there were four inches of Tessa's belongings rising above the lid line, and she'd still been pulling stuff out of her drawers. Dad said it was because she'd been in and out of so many foster homes, she was used to taking everything she owned with her wherever she went.

And Mom's complaining about me carrying a couple of journals, Lily thought.

But she had to reconsider that as she climbed the back stairs to change her jeans. It wasn't that Mom, or Dad, or even Tessa, or Lily's brothers, Joe and Art, actually *complained* about her spiritual stuff—like keeping journals and lighting candles and dropping off and picking up dirt in their travels. It was more that they didn't *understand* it, except for Dad, and he wasn't going with them to Paris.

And neither was the only other person who "got it."

Lily squinted through the dim upstairs hall light at the clock, which was barely visible against the faded-daffodil wallpaper. She still had time to run across the street to St. Margaret's and see Sister Benedict before Kimble and Ingram showed up to say good-bye.

She made a move toward her bedroom door to tell Mom, but she could hear her in there, coaxing Tessa in a voice that was balancing on a tightrope of patience. Not a good time to interrupt. She considered asking Dad, but he was at the bank, getting some Euros so they wouldn't have to exchange money when they first arrived in Paris.

I just got used to pounds and shillings here, Lily thought, as she headed for the boys' room. *Now it's Euros, for Pete's sake — one more reason to stay here instead of running off to France for a month.*

Lily shook her mane of red hair and with it shook off that thought and the dozen others that always followed like little cars on a toy train. *Save it for Sister Benedict,* she told herself. *She'll keep you from becoming a train wreck.*

The boys' door was ajar, and it was obvious that Joe, her eleven-year-old brother, wasn't in there, because it was as quiet as a British bank — and *that* was quiet. People in England, Lily had found, always talked in whispers around money.

But the quiet didn't mean her eighteen-year-old brother, Art, w*asn't* in there. In fact, the more deathly silent a room was, the more likely Art was occupying it, especially today. He was in one of his moods.

Lily took a deep breath, steeled herself for possible projectiles, and tapped on the door.

"What?" came the voice from within.

Lily pushed the door open and flashed a smile so forced it hurt her lips. Art didn't see it. He was lying on his back on one of the sagging twin beds. His short, curly red hair was brilliant against the dingy pillowcase, his hands folded over his chest, and his eyes closed. At least he didn't look as if he were going to pick up the bedside lamp and hurl it at her.

"Could you give Mom a message for me?" Lily said.

Art answered in a voice soaked in contempt. "If I see her."

How could you not see her? Lily thought. *She checks on you every seven seconds, for heaven's sake.* If it wasn't to make sure his blood sugar wasn't too far up or too far down, it was to try to pull him out of a black mood or make sure he wasn't about to spiral down into one.

Lily had thought more than once that it was no wonder Art got irritable. Between finding out he had a disease called diabetes and having Mom hover over him in very un-Mom-like fashion, he pretty much had a right to be cranky as far as Lily was concerned.

Lily softened a little. "I'm bummed out too," she said. "I'm sure Paris is going to be great and all that, but I've got friends here."

"Bully for you," Art said. "I've got friends back in Jersey—"

"Well, so do I—"

"Who are right now packing to go to State Finals with the jazz band *I* started," Art moaned. "One more thing I've had to give up because of this stupid disease, so don't go there with me, all right?"

He opened one blue eye just wide enough to glare at her like some kind of pirate. Lily felt all sympathy fade away.

"Sorry," she said. "Would you just tell Mom I'm going to see Sister Benedict, and I'll be back in time to leave for the train station?"

"Whatever," Art said, and let his eye slam shut again.

Lily went downstairs to the kitchen, scribbled a note to Mom, and leaned it against the goodies for the train that were stacked on the table. Somebody was bound to see it there.

It was starting to drizzle again as Lily crossed busy Woodstock Road. She pulled up the hood of her rain jacket and charged ahead. She was used to rain, cars going down the "wrong" side of the road, and everyone speaking in clipped, proper-sounding tones. Some people even told her she was starting to sound rather British herself.

But one thing that never ceased to amaze her was St. Margaret's, and all the other churches in England that she had visited, for that matter. They were so seasoned with age and holy looking, inside and out.

Lily ran her hand across the pale stone of St. Margaret's wall as she cut a corner amid the tall trees that bent over the peaked roof. She could almost feel the prayers of centuries of people who had entered before her, right there in the cold, damp stone. She always sensed them, as she did now, passing under the covered walkway where the statue of Christ looked down from his cross. Even as she pushed open the heavy door, she could hear Sister Benedict in her head, reminding her that God wasn't only in the churches.

Remember where he spoke to you in London, she would say, her eyes murky-brown with age, twinkling in her cobwebby face.

158

Lily *did* remember. But the churches, especially St. Margaret's, were still special places to her, filled with their holy silence. Besides, this was where she had first discovered her pilgrimage guide.

And then as if Lily had called ahead for a reservation, Sister Benedict stepped out from a row of chairs on the slate floor into the shaft of light Lily let in as she entered. The old woman smiled so that the whole cobweb of lines danced to life.

"How do you always know when I'm coming?" Lily said.

Sister Benedict cupped a gnarled hand around her ear. "You were humming? What were you humming? I don't hear so well, you know."

Ya think? Lily thought. But she just smiled at her Anglican-nun friend and tucked her arm through the frail woman's elbow draped in her gray flannel cape. Though it was spring-warm outside, there was always a chill in the church. Lily was anxious to get to Sister Benedict's cozy cell of a room where there would be an inviting cup of tea, sunlight streaming through the tiny window, and the glow of candle flames to make her feel warm.

Once they were settled in her cell, Sister Benedict looked at Lily over the top of her nose, which reminded Lily of a cone full of marbles. "So this is your last day in Oxford for a while. I trust you've a good deal of worry about that."

"It's only for a month!" Lily said, and then she sagged. "A whole month. Am I an ungrateful little creep for not being happy that I get to go to Paris?"

"Ah, Lily, love. Drink your tea and think about what you've just said. Does our good God make 'creeps'?"

Lily sipped. She could practically feel the freckles on her forehead folding as she creased it. "I guess not," she said. "It's just that, for one thing, I'll miss Dad. We're getting along again, you know, after all the stuff that happened in December. And he understands my pilgrimage too. Not that Mom's mean about it or anything. I just don't always think she exactly *gets* it, especially since she has to spend so much time worrying about Art." Lily stopped for a breath. "He's in one of his funks again."

Sister Benedict nodded. "I expect it's very difficult for him."

159

"Yeah, and when it's difficult for him, it's difficult for the rest of us. It's like he can frost up an entire room just by coming in—another reason I'm not looking forward to this trip. Nobody has much fun when he's all frozen-up like that. He used to be so cool—I mean—not that I don't still love him—I mean—he's my brother, but right now it's hard to *like* him. Is that bad, you know, with him having diabetes and everything? Should I just understand him, spit spot, just like that?"

Lily dusted her hands together, and Sister Benedict chuckled in her young-sounding way.

"You are not Mary Poppins, Lily, love, and if you were, I suspect I wouldn't be able to bear being 'round you."

"Then forget her!"

Lily watched as Sister Benedict struck a match against the rough-hewn table and lit one in the line of candles that was always present there.

"A prayer for Art," the sister murmured. "Come, Holy Spirit, come."

Lily closed her eyes and whispered yes. But the prayer wouldn't stay in her head.

"It isn't just Art anyway," she said when Sister Benedict had opened her eyes again. "I know I have a better attitude about going to Paris than I did about coming here."

"Ah, yes, I remember."

"But I'm still kind of nervous about a whole new place. What if I get homesick again? What if Kimble and Ingram find new friends to replace me once I'm out of the country? What if they figure out they'd rather just be the two of them and shut me out when I come back?"

Sister Benedict blinked, lit match in hand. "I hardly know which to light a candle for first, Lily, love." She touched the flame to wicks as she named them off. "Homesick. Missing Ingram. Missing Kimble." She chuckled as she shook out the match just before it began to singe her fingertips. "I don't think we need to pray that Ingram and Kimble will not become a twosome in your absence. I should imagine it would be more likely that the queen will take up belly dancing."

Lily snickered. Maybe that was stretching her anxiety a little. With Ingram being all about the ages of castles and the dates of kings and Kimble being all about cosmetics and available blokes — boys — they probably weren't going to run off together while Lily wasn't looking.

Besides, Lily and Ingram were thirteen-looking-at-fourteen, and Kimble was a year older. The thought of dating somebody, much less teaming up for life, wasn't in the near future in Lily's mind *or* Ingram's. She knew that. Kimble would have said it was, but Lily knew better. A lot of what Kimble did and said was to protect herself from all the things she had to deal with at home. Dad and Mom had explained that to Lily.

She looked up from the dancing candle flames to see Sister Benedict watching her with that I-know-what-you're-thinking look on her face. Lily knew she probably did.

"It wouldn't be this hard," Lily said, "if I didn't feel like all my friends back home had fallen off the face of the earth."

"You've still not heard from Reni?"

Lily shook her head, and she could feel her heart dipping down to meet her stomach. "She hasn't emailed me in two weeks. The only person who emails me anymore is Mudda—you know, my grandmother. And she tells me stuff like 'don't forget to go barefoot once a day no matter where you are,' and 'write down one important thing that happens every day.'"

"Wise old crone, that Mudda."

"I get an email once a week from Suzy, but that's just Suzy. She probably does it like a homework assignment. Kresha doesn't have a computer, and Zooey only writes her *name* when she absolutely has to. But Reni." Lily swallowed the lump in her throat. "She's my best friend. At least, I thought she was."

Sister Benedict kept nodding as she lit another candle. Now the little cell was flooded with light, and Lily could better see the smile that always made her want to smile too, no matter what was happening. Sister Benedict's funny thin hair and the shelf her ample bosom made across her chest made Lily want to burst into guffaws sometimes. But the sister's smile brought on genuine joy. Right now, however, it was bringing tears to Lily's eyes.

"Why does everything have to change all the time?" Lily burst out. Her breath snuffed out one of the candle flames.

"Ah, Lily, love." Sister Benedict carefully picked up the matchbook and slowly relit the wick. "Change will happen whether we stay where we are or move about. That is life itself." She peered keenly at Lily, the candlelight flickering, wisdom-like, in her eyes. "Especially when one is on a pilgrimage with the Lord, as you are."

"But you're my pilgrimage guide! How am I supposed to go on without you?"

"You can't go on unless you *aren't* with me. It's time you let God be your guide." She put up her hand before Lily could even open her mouth to protest. "You know how to do that. He has shown you again and again."

Lily gnawed on a thumbnail. "I can do it *here,* because I know this place now. But everything's going to be different in France."

"Indeed it will. Different language, different food, different customs—different things you haven't even imagined. If you should feel awkward and silly, and you will, just get quiet and feel God's presence. He will show you what to do." Sister Benedict's eyes twinkled amber in the light. "Besides, it is a good thing for all of us to feel rather stupid from time to time, just to keep us humble."

Lily felt herself scowling. If this was supposed to make her feel better, it wasn't working. Her heart sunk further into the "anxiety zone" deep in her stomach. She set her tea aside.

"Then I guess I feel pretty humble right now."

"But that is the joy of it, love! There will be no dull sameness in your life. What is it Kimble says about hers?"

"It's wet," Lily said. Kimble had been instrumental in the development of Lily's slang vocabulary since she'd come to England.

"However," Sister Benedict said. She held up a knotty old finger. "It wouldn't matter if you traveled to Paris and Rome and Tokyo or stayed right here in Oxford. Once you are on such a pilgrimage as yours, you will continue to change. You are shedding that false self and finding the true soul God gave you."

"Tell me again how I'm supposed to keep finding me?" Lily said. "I know you told me a hundred million times, but right now I'm all confused again. See, that's why I need you—"

Sister Benedict put her finger to her own lips. It was, Lily knew, her kind way of saying, *Shut up, Lily.*

"You look for the sacred all around you," she said when Lily was quiet.

"And not just in the churches, right?" Lily whispered.

"Not just in the churches. Although I'm told you don't want to miss Notre Dame. Magnificent cathedral." Sister Benedict gave a nod. "Look in God's details, Lily. You will see him at work showing you what he wants you to do. That is what Jesus did. That is where you will find both God and yourself."

They both gazed for a long moment into the candles. Lily could feel herself calming down, feel her heart returning to its normal place, feel God's Spirit working within her.

And then the moment was splattered like a foot in a puddle by someone knocking enthusiastically on the door.

"Hey, Sister B—is Lily in there?"

Lily rolled her eyes. It was Tessa. *I bet I could hide in Fort Knox and she'd find a way to get in,* Lily thought. *Of course, I did leave that big old honkin' note on the table.*

Sister Benedict called to Tessa to come in, which she did with more noise than the convent halls had probably heard in centuries, Lily was sure.

"Would you shush?" Lily said.

"Okay," Tessa whispered in a voice about as soft as a foghorn. "Mom says you gotta come home—it's almost time to leave for the train station. And Dad wants to check everybody for the billionth time to make sure we all have our passport thingies." She turned then to Sister Benedict, her big green eyes glowing in the light. "We're goin' to Paris today."

"Are you now?"

"My mom's gonna show some missionary over there how to teach street kids to be physically fit and stuff like that."

"It's a fine ministry your mother has."

Tessa cocked her head of short, wavy, dark hair. "Mom's not a minister."

"Indeed she is. Everyone has a ministry, Tessa my pet. Even you."

"That's a scary thought," Lily said. "Come on, Tess. We better go."

Tessa leaned lazily against Lily's arm. "We got some time. Just as I was leavin', Art started havin' one of those insult things."

"He insulted Mom?"

"He assaulted your mother?"

Tessa looked at both of them in disgust. "No — one of those things where he starts talking like he's drunk and gettin' the shakes, and you have to give him orange juice or somethin'."

"An *insulin* reaction!" Lily said. She turned to Sister Benedict, who still looked bewildered with her hand cupped around her ear. "When he takes his insulin medicine but doesn't eat enough, he has this weird reaction. One time Dad *and* Joe had to hold him down while Mom poured juice down his throat."

"He doesn't take care of himself like he's supposed to," Tessa said, sounding exactly like Mom.

"I think I shall keep his candle lit for a while then," Sister Benedict said. "And the rest —" She bent her head toward the candles.

"Let me put 'em out!" Tessa said. She grabbed for the snuffer and then let it clatter back to the table. "I mean, could I?"

"I wish you would."

Sister Benedict smiled and Lily cringed as Tessa pressed the snuffer's cone over each flame, gushing wax around its sides and sending smoke all over the tiny cell. But Lily knew what the smile was for. Tessa was saying the words along with the two of them: "Let the light of Jesus be in our hearts today, O God, our Father, and let it guide our way."

When the last candle was put out, Tessa looked up at the smoke-filled room and said, "That rocks."

"Amen," Sister Benedict said. "Now off with you." She gave Lily a sly smile. "Go on, now, spit spot."

If Tessa had ever even seen *Mary Poppins,* she didn't let on. She bolted out of the room with the same clatter she'd come in with. Lily turned to Sister Benedict with her chin trembling.

"No tears now, Lily, love," Sister said as she wrapped her arms around her. "Just a hug — and this."

She let Lily out of her broad-shouldered squeeze and pressed a lumpy bundle into Lily's hand.

"Put this in that pilgrimage satchel your grandmother gave you," she said. "You'll need it on the journey, I should think."

Lily fought back tears and nodded. And then there didn't seem to be anything to do but go. As she hurried through St. Margaret's, she whispered, "Here I go again, God. Please promise me you'll be there."

But she heard only the holy silence.

Chapter 2

"All right, I need to take roll call," Mom said. "Art—passport?"

Art didn't answer. He just held up the little blue booklet and grunted.

"Lil—passport?"

Lily pulled her eyes away from the bevy of creamy-skinned children who were all chattering away in what she could only assume was French. Almost everyone in the airport, including the person on the intercom, was speaking in sentences that had a lilt at the end of each, a small lifting up that made her want to raise her eyebrows. But somehow it seemed doubly unusual to hear it coming from little kids.

"Yo—Lil."

"Here!"

"Do you have your passport?" Mom said.

"Yes. It's in my backpack."

"I want to see it with my own eyes. Joe?"

"Here—yeah, I got it—looky-looky."

Joe waved his passport a few inches from Mom's face.

She gave him a look. "Tess?"

"I'm here. It's that blue thing, right?"

One of Mom's eyebrows went up.

"I *think* I got it—" Tessa said.

"Aw, man, tell me you didn't lose it," Joe said. "Mom, you oughta carry it for her, dude."

Mom's other eyebrow lifted. "If we ever get separated, you each need to be carrying your own passport for identification. Tess, you need to find it or you don't get past those guys in uniform." She pointed at two burly men dressed in black and white who looked as if they had long ago forgotten how to smile.

"I got it," Tessa said. She revealed her big front teeth in a grin. "I was just messin' with ya."

"Those dudes will mess with *you*," Joe said. "I saw a show once where they wrestled some guy to the ground and broke one of his arms 'cause he was jokin' about havin' a bomb in the airport."

"Don't *even* go there," Mom said. "Just show me those passports."

Both Lily and Tessa waved theirs, and the group was once again under way. Lily figured the "dudes" in the black and white uniforms must feel sorry for Mom because they didn't search any of their luggage or ask any questions. Lily was relieved.

Joe had done nothing but talk the whole way on the train from Oxford and the plane from London about shows he'd seen where security guards tortured suspected terrorists. He'd had Lily biting her nails over whether they'd think the little baggie of dirt in her suitcase was some kind of explosive.

"Wait for me just on the other side of that wall," Mom called to Art as he grabbed his suitcase off the belt. "The Edwards are meeting us there."

"Who are the Edwards again?" Tessa said.

"You got a head like a colander," Joe said. "Everything goes right through it."

"They're that American family that lives here and helps out people on missions," Lily said.

"Will they be able to speak English?" Tessa asked.

"They're Americans, lame-o," Joe said.

Lily glanced back as the three of them pulled their suitcases off the belt. Mom was too far away to have heard that, or Lily knew she would have been all over Joe. They weren't really supposed to call each other names. But traveling seemed to bring out the worst in everyone. She sighed. This could be a long month.

They rounded the wall Mom had told Art about, and there he was, plastered against it by a rounded man and woman with smiles the size of Montana and hair the color of London fog. Lily could hear them talking far above the hum of the airport bustle.

Yikes, Lily thought. *Nobody else is that loud.*

At least there would be somebody making more noise than Tessa.

"This *has* to be the rest of your family!" the woman said as Tessa, Joe, and Lily reached Art. She put her dimpled hand to her cheek with its round splotch of blush. "What a precious little family! Bless your hearts!"

Everything about Mrs. Edwards had an exclamation point attached to it, Lily thought. Including her hair, which was swept up in the back and obviously sprayed into place. Otherwise, it was defying the law of gravity. Lily looked anxiously at Tessa. If she was true to form, she'd be saying something about that hairdo in the next seven seconds.

"Dan Edwards," the man was saying as he shook Joe's hand so hard the kid's heels came off the ground. He was grinning clown-lines into his face. "This is my wife, Betty."

Before Lily could even say hi, Betty Edwards had her arms around Lily and was squeezing the breath out of her.

"It is so *good* to have other Americans here," she said. Her peppermint breath was hot against Lily's ear. "We are just thrilled to have you."

She turned her attention to Joe, who backed up as if she were a python. Tessa leaned against Lily and whispered, "We aren't staying with *them,* are we?"

Lily just shook her head at Tessa and tried to look pleasant. Somebody had to. Joe was making no attempt to hide his disgust at Betty's gushing and hugging. Tessa was surveying Dan as if he were a suspect in a lineup. And Art, of course, was glowering until his eyebrows practically touched his chin.

"It was nice of you to meet us," Lily said.

Tessa pinched her hard on the back of the arm.

"Bless your heart—it is absolutely our joy!" Betty said. "And we've hired a limo. We knew we'd never fit all of you and your luggage into our little ol' car, and you just don't do the Metro."

"What's the Metro and why don't we do it?" Tessa asked. She sounded like she was conducting a police interrogation.

Betty and Dan wrinkled their noses in unison. "It's the subway—you know, under the ground," Betty said. She lowered her voice to a hoarse whisper. "And, bless their hearts, the people here don't wear deodorant. It gets a little—you know—" She finished the sentence by holding her nose.

"I don't wear deodorant, either," Tessa said.

Betty's wide, exclamation-point eyes popped open. Beside her, Dan's jaw was dropping.

"She's only ten," Lily said. "She doesn't need it yet."

"I don't stink," Tessa said.

To Lily's immense relief, Mom appeared just then, her hand already extended to Dan. Lily had to smother a giggle when Dan grabbed it and pumped it up and down with more enthusiasm than Mom was obviously expecting.

Tessa looked up at Lily, mouth poised for comment. Lily poked her in the ribs with her elbow to keep her from embarrassing all of them. All she said was, "Ow!"

"Are we all together then?" Betty said, after she squeezed Mom around the neck until Lily thought she would turn blue. "Bless your hearts—you must be exhausted."

"I'm not," Tessa said. "I wanna see Paris."

"You will, kiddo!" Dan spoke with his share of exclamation points too. "Betts and I are at your disposal. Any time you want a tour, all you have to do is say the word."

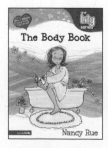

Lily and the Creep (Book Three)

Softcover • ISBN-10: 0-310-23252-X
ISBN-13: 978-0-310-23252-0

Lily learns what it means to be a child of God
and how to develop God's image in herself.

The Buddy Book

Softcover • ISBN-10: 0-310-70064-7
ISBN-13: 978-0-310-70064-7
(Companion Nonfiction to *Lily and the Creep*)

The Buddy Book is all about relationships—why they're important,
how lousy your life can be if they're crummy, what makes a good
one, and how God is the Counselor for all of them.

Lily's Ultimate Party (Book Four)

Softcover • ISBN-10: 0-310-23253-8
ISBN-13: 978-0-310-23253-7

After Lily's plans for the "ultimate" party fall apart, her grandmother shows
Lily that having a party for the right reasons will help to make it a success.

The Best Bash Book

Softcover • ISBN-10: 0-310-70065-5
ISBN-13: 978-0-310-70065-4
(Companion Nonfiction to *Lily's Ultimate Party*)

The Best Bash Book provides fun party ideas and alternatives,
as well as etiquette for hosting and attending parties.

Ask Lily (Book Five)

Softcover • ISBN-10: 0-310-23254-6
ISBN-13: 978-0-310-23254-4

Lily becomes the "Answer Girl" and gives
anonymous advice in the school newspaper.

The Blurry Rules Book

Softcover • ISBN-10: 0-310-70152-X
ISBN-13: 978-0-310-70152-1
(Companion Nonfiction to *Ask Lily*)

Explaining ethics for an 8-12 year old girl! You will discover that although there
may not always be an easy answer or a concrete rule, there's always a God answer.

Available now at your local bookstore!

zonder**kidz**

Lily the Rebel (Book Six)

Softcover • ISBN-10: 0-310-23255-4
ISBN-13: 978-0-310-23255-1

Lily starts to question the rules at home and at school and
decides she may not want to follow the rules.

The It's MY Life Book

Softcover • ISBN-10: 0-310-70153-8
ISBN-13: 978-0-310-70153-8

(Companion Nonfiction to *Lily the Rebel*)
The It's MY Life Book is designed to help you find balance in
your struggle for independence, so you can become not only
your best self, but most of all your God-intended self.

Lights, Action, Lily! (Book Seven)

Softcover • ISBN-10: 0-310-70249-6
ISBN-13: 978-0-310-70249-8

Cast in a Shakespearean play at school by a mere fluke, Lily is immediately
convinced she's destined for a career on Broadway, but finally learns through
a series of entanglements that relationships are more important than a perfect
performance.

The Creativity Book

Softcover • ISBN-10: 0-310-70247-X
ISBN-13: 978-0-310-70247-4

(Companion Nonfiction to *Lights, Action, Lily!*)
Discover your creativity and learn to enjoy the arts in
this fun, activity-filled book written by Nancy Rue.

Lily Rules! (Book Eight)

Softcover • ISBN-10: 0-310-70250-X
ISBN-13: 978-0-310-70250-4

Lily is voted class president at her school, but unlike her
predecessors who have been content to sail along with the title and a
picture in the yearbook, Lily is out to make changes.

The Uniquely Me Book

Softcover • ISBN- 10: 0-310-70248-8
ISBN- 13: 978-0-310-70248-1

(Companion Nonfiction to *Lily Rules!*)
At some point, every girl wonders why she was born and why she's the
way she is. Well, author Nancy Rue has written the perfect book designed
to answer all those nagging uncertainties from a biblical perspective.

Available now at your local bookstore!

zonder**kidz**

Rough & Rugged Lily (Book Nine)

Softcover • ISBN-10: 0-310-70260-7
ISBN-13: 978-0-310-70260-3

Lily's convinced she's destined to become a great outdoorswoman, but when the Robbins family is stranded in a snowstorm on the way to a mountain cabin to celebrate Christmas, she learns the real meaning of survival and how dependent she is on the material things of life.

The Year 'Round Holiday Book

Softcover • ISBN-10: 0-310-70256-9
ISBN-13: 978-0-310-70256-6
(Companion Nonfiction to *Rough and Rugged Lily*)
The Year 'Round Holiday Book will help you celebrate traditional holidays with not only fun and pizzazz, but with deeper meaning as well.

Lily Speaks! (Book Ten)

Softcover • ISBN-10: 0-310-70262-3
ISBN-13: 978-0-310-70262-7

Lily enters the big speech contest at school and learns the up and downsides of competition through her pain and disappointment, as well as the surprise benefits, and how God heals jealousy, envy, and self-doubt.

The Values & Virtues Book

Softcover • ISBN-10: 0-310-70257-7
ISBN-13: 978-0-310-70257-3
(Companion Nonfiction to *Lily Speaks!*)
The Values & Virtues Book offers you tips and skills for improving your study habits, sportsmanship, relationships, and every area of your life.

Available now at your local bookstore!

zonderkidz

Horse Crazy Lily (Book Eleven)
Softcover • ISBN-10: 0-310-70263-1
ISBN-13: 978-0-310-70263-4

Lily's in love! With horses?! Back in the "saddle" for another exciting adventure, Lily's gone western and feels she's destined to be the next famous cowgirl.

The Fun-Finder Book
Softcover • ISBN-10: 0-310-70258-5
ISBN-13: 978-0-310-70258-0
(Companion Nonfiction to *Horse Crazy Lily*)

The Fun-Finder Book is designed to help you find out what you like so that you can develop your own just-for-you hobby. And if you just can't figure it out, a self-quiz helps you recognize your likes and dislikes as you discover your God-given talent.

Lily's Church Camp Adventure (Book Twelve)
Softcover • ISBN-10: 0-310-70264-X
ISBN-13: 978-0-310-70264-1

Lily learns a real lesson about the essential habits of the heart when she and the Girlz attend Camp Galilee.

The Walk-the-Walk Book
Softcover • ISBN-10: 0-310-70259-3
ISBN-13: 978-0-310-70259-7
(Companion Nonfiction to *Lily's Church Camp Adventure*)

Every young girl needs the training that develops positive and lifelong spiritual habits. Prayer, Bible study, devotion, simplicity, confession, worship, and celebration are foundational spiritual disciplines to help you "walk-the-walk."

Lily's in London?! (Book Thirteen)
Softcover • ISBN-10: 0-310-70554-1
ISBN-13: 978-0-310-70554-3

Lily's London adventures strengthen her relationship with God as she realizes, more than ever, there are many possibilities for walking her spiritual path in Christ.

Lily's Passport to Paris (Book Fourteen)
Softcover • ISBN-10: 0-310-70555-X
ISBN-13: 978-0-310-70555-0

Lily visits Paris and meets Christophe, an orphan boy at the mission where her mom is working. While helping Christophe to understand who God is, Lily finally discovers her own mission. This last book in the series also includes a letter from Nancy Rue, which tells what happens to the characters after the series ends, and introduces the character of Sophie LaCroix from the Faithgirlz! Sophie Series.

Available now at your local bookstore!

zonder**kidz**

Own the entire collection of Lily fiction and companion nonfiction books by Nancy Rue!

Lily Fiction Titles	Companion Nonfiction Title
Here's Lily!, Book One	The Beauty Book
Lily Robbins, M.D., Book Two	The Body Book
Lily and the Creep, Book Three	The Buddy Book
Lily's Ultimate Party, Book Four	The Best Bash Book
Ask Lily, Book Five	The Blurry Rules Book
Lily the Rebel, Book Six	The It's MY Life Book
Lights, Action, Lily!, Book Seven	The Creativity Book
Lily Rules!, Book Eight	The Uniquely Me Book
Rough & Rugged Lily, Book Nine	The Year-Round Holiday Book
Lily Speaks!, Book Ten	The Values & Virtues Book
Horse Crazy Lily, Book Eleven	The Fun-Finder Book
Lily's Church Camp Adventure, Book Twelve	The Walk-the-Walk Book
Lily's in London?!, Book Thirteen	
Lily's Passport to Paris, Book Fourteen	

Available now at your local bookstore!

zonder**kidz**

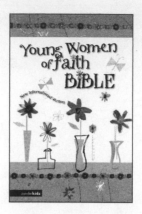

NIV Young Women of Faith Bible

General Editor: Susie Shellenberger

Hardcover • ISBN-10: 0-310-91394-2
ISBN-13: 978-0-310-91394-8

Softcover • ISBN-10: 0-310-70278-X
ISBN-13: 978-0-310-70278-8

Now there is a study Bible designed especially for
girls ages 8 to 12. Created to develop a habit of studying God's
Word in young girls, the *NIV Young Women of Faith Bible* is full of
cool, fun to read in-text features that are not only interesting, but
provide insight. It has 52 weekly studies thematically tied to the
NIV Women of Faith Study Bible to encourage a special time of
study for mothers and daughters to share in God's Word.

Available now at your local bookstore!

We want to hear from you. Please send your comments
about this book to us in care of zreview@zondervan.com. Thank you.

Grand Rapids, MI 49530
www.zonderkidz.com

ZONDERVAN.com/
AUTHORTRACKER
follow your favorite authors